THE UNANSWERED QUESTION

I caught up with him between classes and asked him who was going with us to the movie that evening.

He didn't answer my question. Instead, he put his arms up against the wall on each side of me and leaned close. "I love looking into your eyes," he said. "Did you know that you have the longest eyelashes I've ever seen?"

I could feel my blush spreading over my face.

"Gotta go," he said and plunged into the crowd without a backward glance.

He left me breathless. And feeling more than a little gawky and stupid. He was like quicksilver, escaping my grasp and leaving me more intrigued than ever . . .

AMELIA

JEAN THESMAN

AN AVON  FLARE BOOK

THE WHITNEY COUSINS: AMELIA is an original publication of Avon Books. This work has never before appeared in book form.

AVON BOOKS
A division of
The Hearst Corporation
105 Madison Avenue
New York, New York 10016

First Avon Flare Printing: May 1990

Chapter 1

Incredibly Intelligent Idea No. 1: Yesterday on a
Metro bus, I discovered that if you say ten times,
"Every day I get smarter and smarter," the other
passengers get off at the next stop.

Mogoo, the Mad Magician

Some people thrive on the excitement of big changes,
but frankly I agree with my friend, Mark Reid. He says,
"Stay away from people like that. They're also probably
picking up radio stations from another planet on the fill-
ings in their teeth." Mark, who plays Mogoo the Magician in the clown troupe, may sound like an idiot
sometimes, but if you listen closely, he makes a certain
kind of sense.

If I could have my way, nothing about my life would
change except the contents of my closet. And I'd give
up new clothes if it meant I'd never, ever have to live
through another time like my sophomore year.

The first devastating change came when my cousin
Heather, my best friend since we were babies, moved
to Fox Crossing, which is miles from Seattle. I started
my new school year without her and felt, for a while, as
if I'd left part of me home every morning.

The next change came when I had a terrifying experience and found out afterward that some of the people
I'd always thought I could count on dropped me faster
than my enemies did. But I didn't have premonitions of
disaster that autumn. I liked all my classes except the

one I had with Miss Lear, who is the world's biggest pain in the elbow. And the best-looking new boy in school was interested in me. What more could anybody want?

One morning at school, my friend Wendy Ingram and I had barely settled ourselves in our seats in first period when she poked my arm and whispered, "Amelia, there he is. Look out the window."

I looked and saw Warren Carey in the driveway, jogging toward the main entrance. Even in a miserable Seattle December, he looked as tan as he had when he started his senior year here in September. His blond hair had been streaked by the faraway California sun. He was tall and lean and gorgeous, and he'd asked me out twice already, but I hadn't been able to accept.

Carl MacArthur, Wendy's boyfriend, leaned over her shoulder while she was still looking out the window. "Good morning, love of my life," he said. "Are you checking out the competition?"

"Oh, you," Wendy said, laughing, and she caught his hand. They were so cute together. They were the same height, but she had soft, curly hair, almost black, and his hair was red. "What are you doing here, Carl?" she demanded. "You'll be late to class."

Carl was a junior. We didn't have classes with him but he often tracked Wendy down, just to say hello. I loved watching them, and I wanted the same sort of relationship for myself. But it wasn't happening. Not yet.

Carl's younger sister Meg was in our class, though. She wasn't a redhead like her brother, but instead had light brown hair like mine. They, along with Wendy and Mark, had put together a wonderful clown act, and even though I wouldn't agree to join them, the five of us were as close as we'd ever been.

Meg gave her brother a teasing shove. "Get going."

2

She slid into the seat behind me. "Amelia, was that Warren outside?"

"Warren, Warren," Carl grumbled on his way to the door. He didn't like the new senior, even though he barely knew him.

Meg scowled at me. "I can't believe that Warren asked you out twice and you turned him down both times."

"I had to," I said. "The first time was when Dad planned the surprise party for Mom's birthday and the second time . . ."

"Was when you helped out at my sister's bridal shower," Wendy said. "Mom really needed you."

"I'm not complaining," I said. "He'll ask me again." But I wasn't certain of that. And I wasn't sure I'd go. There was something about him that bothered me, something I couldn't explain to myself. I'd even written to Heather in Fox Crossing about him. He was—I don't know—different from the other boys. He watched me too much, and sometimes his expression was too *knowing*.

Miss Lear, our ugly English teacher, strolled in then. Meg scuttled back to her seat and I bent quickly to pull my notebook out of my book bag. The class was so silent that I could hear the other kids breathing. The bell rang but Miss Lear didn't sit down at her desk. She looked us over with her mean little eyes.

"Amelia Whitney, read the bulletin," she said.

I got up and hurried toward the front of the class, brushing nervously at my new skirt, the one Mom and I had made in our sewing class at the community center. Miss Lear knew how much I hated reading the bulletin, so she called on me the most often.

She watched me picking at my skirt. "Did you make that skirt yourself?" she asked.

"My mother helped me," I said.

"Hmm," she murmured. She handed me the bulletin.

3

I was in agony. This was the first time I'd worn the skirt and I'd thought that it looked wonderful. But now I wasn't so sure. I looked down at it and then up at Miss Lear. She was smiling, but the smile didn't reach her eyes.

"Well?" she cooed with nasty sweetness. "Are you going to read or shall I ask someone to help you with the hard words?"

I could feel my face burning as I stammered through the bulletin. I hated her, hated her, hated her, but only half as much as Wendy did. They'd been enemies for months.

My ears rang for the first half hour of the class, and I spent the last of it wishing that I knew a way to keep myself from getting bent out of shape over Miss Lear practically every day. The bell rang and I nearly jumped up and down with relief.

Wendy pulled a permission slip out of her notebook and said, "I have to get this PS signed. You don't need to wait."

"I don't mind," I said.

I watched while she approached Miss Lear. "My PS has to be signed today," Wendy said. "Remember, I spoke to you about . . ."

Miss Lear stared down at the paper. "What's this?"

"It's the permission slip I told you about. We're taking the clown act to two grade schools for their Christmas programs, and all the other teachers . . ."

"Put it on my desk and I'll get around to it," Miss Lear said.

"But . . ."

Miss Lear strolled out of the room, heading for the teachers' lounge. She didn't look back.

"Oh, darn!" Wendy exclaimed angrily. "She's done it to me again!"

"She only likes boys," Meg said. "Don't let her get to you."

4

"But what am I going to do if she doesn[...] How did you get her to sign yours?"

"I had Carl bring it in after school one aftern[...] week when she was in a hurry to leave," Meg [...]. "But that won't work for you. She knows he dates you and I'm only his sister."

"Go anyway," I said. "What's the worst that can happen?"

"I don't know," Wendy said angrily. "The end of the world, probably." She left the slip in the center of Miss Lear's desk, where she'd be sure to see it, and stomped out of the room with Meg and me trailing behind.

I was astonished to see Warren waiting outside the door. He smiled at me and linked his arm with mine. "I wondered how long you were going to stay in there."

I swallowed hard. Wendy and Meg had disappeared tactfully, and I couldn't think of anything to say.

"Where's your next class?" Warren asked.

I told him, but he shook his head. "I have to go in the opposite direction," he said. "You've got first lunch?"

"Second," I croaked. Everyone was watching us, and I'd never felt more self-conscious. Was my skirt really horrible? Probably.

"We could sit together if you had first lunch," Warren said. He stepped back and grinned at me. "I love green eyes. You are really one cute girl," he said. "See you around."

He was gone and I could start breathing again. Talking to him always made me nervous. I was never certain if I was saying the right thing. I took off, hurrying as much as I dared in the crowded hall, and skimmed around the corner and into my next class just as the bell rang. Wendy and Meg were already in their places, giggling over Meg's newest drawing.

Mrs. Nugent, the art teacher, nodded briskly to me as I took my place at the table next to Mark, a tall, dark

5

..r and Carl's best friend. He nudged me companionably and grinned. "Your hair's a mess," he said. "Did you comb it with a ceiling fan?"

"Thanks," I grumbled, but I pulled my fingers through my stubborn mop, trying to tame it. I could always count on Mark to comment about something. He'd probably point to my skirt next and start laughing.

"You tangled with Lear again, didn't you?" he asked. "Why don't you just ignore her? Pretend you don't hear her."

"Keep your advice to yourself, oh mouthpiece of the gods," I hissed. Boys never understood what a witch Miss Lear was.

"Only trying to help," he whispered as the teacher walked up and down between the tables, passing out graded sketches.

I saw the A on the corner of mine and breathed a big sigh of relief. At least things turned out right in this class. But Mark burst out laughing when he saw his grade, and Mrs. Nugent turned back to stare at him.

"What does a question mark stand for?" Mark asked.

"It means," she told him, "that I don't know what to do with somebody who draws wonderful cartoon characters when I asked for a city scene demonstrating what you know about perspective."

"Don't clown around," I whispered, but it was too late.

"How about H for hopeless?" he asked. "Or maybe W for weird?"

"Next time it'll be X for exasperating," Mrs. Nugent said. "Behave yourself or I'll change my mind about letting you out of class two days in a row. You do enough clowning in here."

We got busy on our new projects. Rain spattered against the windows, and I could hear the choir rehearsing down the hall. Nice. Christmas was coming and my mind wandered to my gift list.

6

"Are you going to go out with Warren Carey?" Mark asked.

My head jerked up. "What business is that of yours?"

"As your oldest pal in the whole world," he began, as he always did when he was going to start nagging again, "take some advice. I can't begin to tell you what a jerk that guy is."

My pencil slipped and I grabbed my eraser. "You don't even know him."

Mark bent his head over his drawing. "Everybody knows him. He makes sure of that."

I snorted. "You're jealous."

"Fat chance," he growled. "I thought you were crazy about Curt Jerome."

"You don't like Curt, either," I said triumphantly, and I treated him to my best glare. "Back off. You're not my brother."

Mark sighed. "I couldn't stand being related to you."

I elbowed him hard enough to send his pencil flying.

Mrs. Nugent drifted by. "Creating a scene again, are you?" she asked Mark.

He held up his paper. "Yes," he said. "How do you like it?"

She studied his drawing. "It's worth the X we were talking about," she said as she moved on, but she was grinning. Everybody liked Mark, even me.

But, as Mrs. Nugent said, he was exasperating, and he meddled too much. Once I had liked Curt Jerome, but he hadn't paid any attention to me, and since Warren moved to Seattle I hadn't given Curt much thought. However, none of that was Mark's business.

When art was over, Mark walked me to my next class, pestering me again about joining the clown troupe, but I only half listened to him. He'd mentioned Curt, and that reminded me that ever since I lost interest in him, he seemed to be interested in me. When I saw him in

7

the halls, he always grinned or nodded or otherwise let me know he'd noticed me. Boys could be so strange.

"What are you thinking about?" Mark demanded. "I know you're not listening to me."

"I was wondering what institution you escaped from," I said, and I ducked into my history class, knowing that I'd left a half-crazy Mark behind me. He couldn't stand not being able to get the last word.

Wendy and Meg were whispering together, and I sat down beside Wendy, curious. "What's up?"

"I went back to Miss Lear, and she said my PS wasn't on her desk and she doesn't know where it is." Wendy looked close to tears. "I have to start all over again getting the teachers to sign, and the first program is tomorrow."

"Tell Mrs. Camp in the office," I said. "She'll fix it."

Wendy wasn't consoled. But by the time the day was over, she had a new slip with all the signatures except Miss Lear's. Again. Miss Lear knew exactly how to make you a basket case.

After school, Wendy, Meg, and I walked to my house together because I lived closest to school, and then they went their separate ways. The rain was still falling, and I could tell by the mud on the porch that our dogs had gone in and out a dozen times. They, and my little sisters and brother, knew how to make my mother a basket case. Someday the little kids would be students of Miss Lear's—and revenge was going to be very sweet.

Six-year-old Cassie opened the door for me. Her glasses were hanging crooked, as usual, and she had chocolate on her face. "How come you're late?" she asked.

"I'm not," I said. "I'm exactly on time."

Mimi, who was five, ran out of the kitchen next, and she, too, was sticky with chocolate.

8

"What are you guys doing?" I asked. "Is Mom in the kitchen?"

"Unfortunately," Mom said as she followed Mimi into the hall. "I'm trying to make a decent batch of fudge brownies."

I dropped my book bag and hung up my coat. "Does this skirt look all right?"

She eyed me carefully. "It's gorgeous. We did a great job. Why do you ask?"

"Miss Lear sneered at it."

"Miss Lear," Mom groaned, in the same voice she would have used if she'd said Black Plague. "I had a teacher just like her. She was ugly and mean, and she had long black hair on her legs. Because of her, I didn't learn to like Shakespeare until I got to college. Let's forget about her."

"A boy called for you," Cassie said. She shoved up her glasses. "I told him you weren't home."

"Who was it?" I asked. "Mark? Carl?"

Cassie shook her head. "Nobody nice," she said.

Mom stared at her. "I didn't hear the phone ring. Who was it, Cassie?"

Cassie scowled darkly. "Nobody nice. He hung up without saying good-bye."

"But what was his name?" I cried.

Cassie and Mimi drew together. "She said," Mimi said, "that it was nobody nice." And together, they marched off to the kitchen.

"They're snubbing me," I told Mom. I had trouble not laughing.

"Whoever it was will call again," Mom said. "But maybe you'd be better off if he didn't. Cassie has an uncanny knack for identifying creeps."

Too bad I didn't have more respect for Cassie's judgment then. The call had come from Warren, and he phoned again a few minutes later, catching me with my mouth full of tough brownie crumbs.

9

"I tried calling you earlier," Warren said. "I thought you were the sort who'd drive straight home like a good girl."

"I walk," I said, after I'd swallowed. "It takes a while."

"Walk," he repeated, laughing a little. I was embarrassed, as if I'd been caught doing something stupid.

"It's only half a mile," I explained. This had to be the silliest conversation I'd ever had with anybody, but I couldn't seem to fix it.

There was a silence on the line. I had a hunch he was laughing again. Finally he said, "I like watching you walk around the halls at school. You're the cutest girl there, but I'll bet you know that."

"I'm really not," I said.

His voice dropped to a whisper. "I think about you a lot. I want to spend some time with you, getting acquainted."

I had goose bumps on my arms. Both my sisters were staring at me from the kitchen table, and it was only a matter of time until one of them started asking me questions about this conversation.

"Why are you calling?" I blurted.

"How about going to a movie Friday night? That's two days away. You haven't already made plans, have you?"

"No. I guess I could go. Just a minute while I ask my mom."

He laughed again, as if I'd said something funny. "Okay."

I held my hand over the mouthpiece so he couldn't hear me talk. "Mom, it's Warren. He's the one who's asked me out before. Is it okay if I go to a movie with him Friday?"

"Who else is going?" she asked. I could tell something was bothering her.

I asked Warren who else would be going with us.

10

"Two other couples," he said. "We haven't settled everything yet, but there'll be a crowd of us. Isn't that all right?"

"Sure. It's fine," I said. My parents weren't enthusiastic about my going out with boys alone yet.

But Mom didn't seem enthusiastic about anything right then. I told her there'd be six of us going together, and for a moment I thought she was going to say that I couldn't go, but finally she said, "He's coming here for you, isn't he?"

I nodded, and then I asked Warren what time he'd pick me up. "Seven is fine," I said, so that Mom could hear.

"Great," Warren said. "Now I've gotta go." And he hung up without saying good-bye.

I replaced the phone slowly. "What's wrong?" I asked Mom.

She wiped crumbs off the table. "Nothing, I guess," she said. "Well, it bothers me that he's a senior, I suppose."

"I'll be sixteen pretty soon," I said.

Mom pushed back her hair and sighed. "I'm having a hard time adjusting to your growing up so fast."

"You've still got the little guys to fuss over."

"Sure," Mom said. But she sounded worried.

My ten-year-old brother, Jamie, crashed through the back door then, and both the dogs came in with him, shaking water all over us. The bad moment passed. I'd been afraid that Mom was going to change her mind and not let me go out with Warren after all.

I was pleased about the way things had turned out. Warren and I were going out at last, and I should have smiled my way through the next two days. But that's not what happened.

That night, when my family and I were on our way home from the grade school music program, our station wagon stopped at a red light right next to a car driven

11

by Warren. He didn't notice me in the back between my little sisters. But I noticed him.

And right next to him sat Val Guthrie. I guess every school has a girl like Val. She wore too much makeup, dated the wrong boys, stayed out too late, and did all the other things that the rest of us wouldn't have been caught dead doing, or if we were caught, our parents would kill us and we'd be dead anyway. I'd always felt sorry for her—but she despised me, and every other girl in the sophomore class.

Why was Warren with Val?

The light turned green and Warren's car shot out ahead of ours. I hoped that my parents hadn't noticed him, or if they had, they wouldn't remember him. And I decided that I was never, ever going to tell anybody that I'd seen him out with Val. Maybe, being new in school, he just didn't know any better.

Chapter 2

Incredibly Intelligent Idea No. 2: Everybody
ought to be afraid to sleep at night. How would
you really know if a bug crawled up your nose?
                    Mogoo, the Mad Magician

Wendy and Meg weren't at school the next morning because they, along with Carl and Mark, were performing their clown act at two grade schools.

Mrs. MacArthur, Carl and Meg's mom, had started the clown act a year before. She was a caterer, specializing in children's birthday parties, and the clown act was the most popular part of her service. The kids began volunteering for school programs, and lately they'd been planning on turning professional, with Mrs. MacArthur's enthusiastic encouragement. They'd asked me to join them, and I'd been tempted, but I was also very self-conscious. I didn't think I'd ever do as good a job as they did.

Miss Lear noted Wendy's absence from first period, of course. She asked me if I knew where she was.

I shrugged and tried to pretend that I didn't know Miss Lear was going to get Wendy in trouble. "I really don't know, exactly," I said.

Miss Lear smiled her too-sweet smile. "Suppose you tell me where you suspect that she might be, then."

The whole class was holding its breath. I was sure everybody knew that Miss Lear hadn't signed Wendy's PS, and Wendy had gone off with the clowns anyway.

"You could ask someone in the office," I said finally. "I'm sure they know."

Miss Lear tilted her head to one side and studied me thoughtfully. "Fritzie, mark Wendy as absent from class," she said without moving her gaze from me.

If Miss Lear had been inclined to like a girl, ever, that girl would have been Fritzie Seton, who was exactly like her. She was sly and sneaky, stirred up trouble just for the fun of it, and kept everybody so tense that they were afraid not to be nice to her. Naturally, Miss Lear had picked her as attendance monitor on the first day of school.

Fritzie smiled her cold, sly smile and marked Wendy absent.

I groaned inwardly. In a million years I'd never understand how someone like Miss Lear could be employed in the same school with funny, lovable Mrs. Nugent.

The kids were back by second lunch, pleased with how their performance had gone, and we celebrated over pizza. I waited until I had a moment alone with Wendy by my locker, though, to tell her that she was going to have an unexcused absence to deal with.

"I'll have another one tomorrow, too," she said, and her face flushed angrily. "I knew it would happen so I told my counselor as soon as we got to school."

"What did he say?" I asked apprehensively. Mr. Depard wasn't famous for understanding even the most simple situation.

"He said he'd take care of it, but you know he's so absentminded that he doesn't even tie his shoes, so I'll probably be in jail tomorrow afternoon." Wendy bit off a huge chunk of her candy bar and couldn't talk anymore, but she nodded her head vigorously to emphasize what she'd said.

At that moment, Warren walked by. He didn't stop,

but he smiled at me. As soon as he was out of sight, I told Wendy that I was going out with him Friday.

"I'm glad you've finally worked it out," she said. "Where are you going? Who are you going with?"

"He said we'd go to a movie with two other couples."

"Who? Seniors?"

"I don't know. I haven't had a chance to ask him."

Wendy squeezed my arm. "Call me first thing Saturday morning and tell me how it went," she said.

Mark and Meg popped up then, and we changed the subject. I watched for Warren all day, hoping to get a chance to ask him exactly who was going with us on Friday, but I only caught a distant glimpse of him. And he didn't call me that night.

The next day, Wendy and Meg were missing from first period again, and Fritzie's nose turned red with joy at marking Wendy absent twice in a row. Mr. Depard had obviously forgotten to straighten things out. I worried about Wendy—but I also worried about me. I needed some answers from Warren or my parents would cross our date off my calendar.

I caught up with Warren between classes and asked him who was going with us to the movie that evening. We moved over to the side of the hall, out of the stream of traffic, so we could have privacy.

He didn't answer my question. Instead, he put his arms up against the wall on each side of me and leaned close. "I love looking into your eyes," he said. "Did you know that you have the longest eyelashes I've ever seen?"

I could feel my blush spreading over my face.

"Gotta go," he said, and he plunged into the crowd without a backward glance.

He left me breathless. And feeling more than a little gawky and stupid. He was like quicksilver, escaping my grasp and leaving me more intrigued than ever.

But I couldn't help wishing that I hadn't seen him with Val. She'd missed the last two days of school, nothing unusual for her, and I was relieved. I couldn't have looked her in the face.

I got home that afternoon to find an empty house. Mom had left me a note on the refrigerator, explaining that she had taken the little guys to the store with her. There was a letter from my cousin Heather on the table, though, and that would keep me company while I ate my after-school snack.

Halfway through the letter, I decided that it wasn't such great company after all. Usually I loved hearing from Heather. We wrote often, especially during the first awful weeks she spent in Fox Crossing with her new stepfather and stepsister, when she was learning to adjust to a different school and a different life, and everything imaginable was going wrong. But this letter answered my letter about Warren, and I didn't like what I read.

"I wish you wouldn't go out with him until you learn why you feel so uneasy about him," Heather wrote. "Trust your instincts. Something must be wrong or you wouldn't feel the way you do."

I folded the letter hastily and stuck it in my pocket. I'd finish reading it tomorrow, I told myself. After my date. Then I'd answer her and tell her how silly I'd been to doubt Warren.

My whole family came home at once, Dad through the back door and Mom and the little guys through the front. The dogs barked, the kids shouted, and Dad, who'd caught a horrible cold, grumbled his way upstairs to take a hot shower and put on his robe and slippers before dinner.

He ended up having his dinner in bed on a tray, with the dogs for company. I set the kitchen table and helped Mom serve my messy little sisters.

"You haven't forgotten that I have a date tonight," I said. Suddenly I was worried about how my family would seem to Warren. Dad sick in bed, my sisters bick-

16

ering with my brother, and the large, shaggy dogs leaping and barking over everything that excited them. And visitors always excited them. I could see infinite possibilities for disaster.

"I haven't forgotten your date," Mom said as she wiped up Mimi's spilled milk. "Mimi, will you please stop spooning milk into your mouth and drink it straight out of the glass?"

"Pig," Jamie said to Mimi. He had tomato sauce on his shirt.

"Hog," Cassie retorted in defense of her sister.

"Mom?" I pleaded. "Do they have to . . ."

"No, but they do," she said. "Calm down. This isn't your first date."

"It's my first date with somebody I haven't known since kindergarten," I grumbled. "He'll be here in an hour, and I haven't had a chance to wash my hair or press my skirt . . ."

"Go," Mom said. "Wash and press. I'll handle the troops."

I ran out of the kitchen before she changed her mind.

Warren was late. By seven-fifteen, I'd decided that he wasn't coming and I was ready to kill myself. At seven-thirty, I wanted to kill him. By seven fifty, when he arrived, I was desperate enough to be grateful.

Mistake No. 1. I should have slammed the door in his face.

I introduced him to Mom, explained about Dad, peeled the little girls off of me, and escaped with him out the front door.

"I don't like dogs very much," he said, sounding annoyed as he brushed dog hair off his pants.

"Sorry," I said.

He didn't open the passenger door for me, but let me scramble in the car by myself. I deliberately pushed away the recollection that Mark had been opening car doors

17

for me since we started high school. But Warren's car was beautiful and so was he, so what the heck, I thought.

Mistake No. 2.

No one else was in the car but us.

"Where are the other kids?" I asked as we pulled out from the curb.

"We're meeting them at the theater," Warren said.

No one waited at the theater for us, but Warren assured me that we'd find them inside. He bought our tickets and we walked into the warm lobby. The movie was just beginning.

"We'd better get into our seats," Warren said. "I hate missing the beginnings of movies."

I did, too, so we found places to sit and I forgot about the people we were supposed to be with.

Afterward, when the movie was over, I said, "Let's look around for the others. They're probably wondering what happened to us."

"They won't wonder," Warren said, steering me toward the door.

"But who are they?" I said, looking back over my shoulder. "Where are they?"

He threw his arm around my shoulders and hugged me. "Maybe they couldn't make it after all."

I stopped and looked up at him. "What?" I asked stupidly.

"Oh, come on, don't be such a baby," he said. "They're somewhere having a good time, like we ought to be doing."

I looked at my watch. "I guess I can stay out a while longer. I don't have to be in until eleven."

"Eleven," he scoffed. "Who's keeping track of the time?"

My mother, I thought nervously. Dad might be sick in bed, but Mom was capable of raising a terrific howl if I was late.

As Warren backed out of the parking place, he smiled

18

and hummed to himself. I asked him where we were going.

"To a special place I know about," he said. Before I could ask anything more, he started talking about the school he'd gone to the year before and the great times he'd had in California. I watched familiar streets flash by the window.

And then some unfamiliar streets.

"Are you sure you know where we're going?" I asked uncomfortably. "I don't think there's a good place to eat in this part of town."

"Who's hungry?" Warren asked, laughing, and he pulled the car into the entrance to an alley and stopped.

The moment the engine died, I realized what an idiot I was. "I don't want to stop here," I said. "This is an awful neighborhood." Actually, I didn't want to stop anywhere—if he wanted what I suspected he wanted. I hardly knew him, and I wasn't ready to kiss him.

He reached for me and pulled me close. "I'm here," he whispered. "You're safe. I won't let the boogie man get you."

I pushed him away. "It's cold. And scary. Let's go."

He grabbed me again, roughly, and kissed me. "I'll warm you up. I know all the ways."

He pushed my jacket off my shoulders with one hand and held me against the seat with his other arm under my chin, pressing hard against my throat.

"Quit that!" I cried, suddenly more frightened than I had ever been before.

"Relax," he said. "Kiss me."

I turned my face away from him and pushed him as hard as I could, but he tightened the pressure against my throat. Muttering something, he yanked at my shirt and I heard the buttons pop.

I was blind with panic then. I grabbed his hair and tried to pull his face away from mine. When he didn't

19

stop touching me, I went crazy with fear and yanked his hair hard.

He swore and I felt a quick, stinging pain along my collarbone before he let me go. I fumbled for the door handle, but he grabbed me again, digging his fingers into my upper arms and pulling me backward. I wrenched loose and somehow I was out the door and running down the alley.

Behind me, the headlights of his car switched on and I heard his engine start. I ran wildly, not worrying about falling, not worrying about anything except getting away from him.

But he didn't follow me. I looked over my shoulder and saw him backing out into the street. I slowed and stopped. I'd reached the far end of the alley, and I drew close to an old building, huddling against the bricks. If Warren circled the block, he'd see me. I crept back into the alley and crouched down behind a pile of boxes. For the first time I noticed that a cold, sharp rain was pelting me and I was soaked.

I waited for what seemed like hours. It was so dark that I couldn't read my watch. I'd never been that cold and wet. And I was a long way from home.

I left the alley finally, determined to find a phone and call home. My mother would go crazy over this. If I hadn't been so scared of the neighborhood I was walking through, I'd have been scared to face Mom.

Three blocks away, in front of a convenience store, I found a broken phone. Inside the store, half a dozen men hung around the counter, and I was afraid to go in and ask to use the phone there. I kept walking.

A car stopped and a man shouted at me, asking if I wanted a ride. I hurried on without answering. He followed and I broke into a run, finally turning up a short flight of steps to a ramshackle house where a light burned on the porch. I hammered on a scarred old door. An old woman pulled the curtain back from the glass and stared out at me, then walked away.

"I need help!" I cried, but she didn't come back.

The car that had been following me was gone, so I hurried out to the sidewalk again, walking, running, walking again, hoping that I was heading north where I'd eventually find familiar streets. I found another phone, but it was broken, too.

At last I reached the edge of the park near my house, and I stumbled into a run again. I didn't dare go through the park, and circling it would take time, so it was another eternity before I saw my house half a block away, with wonderful lights burning all over.

What was I going to tell Mom? What would she do? What would she think of me?

I couldn't bear to explain what had happened. I just wanted to be inside, safe and warm, and forget everything. If I forgot, then I could stay the way I had been. Safe. Safe.

I tiptoed up the porch steps and let myself in the door. I heard Dad coughing upstairs and Mom talking to him. The little guys were asleep, and the dogs greeted me silently, stretching and yawning. I hurried up the stairs, and from the door of my room, I called out, "I'm home, Mom." I shut the door and began pulling off my clothes.

Mom came to the door and my heart hammered so loud that I could barely hear her. "Did you have a good time?" she asked, without opening the door.

"It was okay," I said, trying to sound exactly the way I always did. My soggy clothes lay in a heap, and I pulled my nightgown over my head. Quick, quick, I thought, before she comes in and sees how wet I got.

But she didn't open the door. "Your dad feels awful," she said. "I'm going to make him a cup of lemon tea. Can I get you anything?"

"No," I said. "I'm tired and want to go to bed. Good night, Mom." I tried to sound cheerful and firm.

" 'Nite, then," she said, and I heard her slippers pad away.

I rolled up my ruined shirt and hid it in the back of the closet. Then I stuffed the rest of my clothes in my hamper and turned out the light. Outside, rain hammered against the window. I shook with cold as I crawled into bed. My upper arms ached and the scratch Warren had made on my collarbone burned.

How could this have happened to me? What had I done that gave Warren the idea he could drive me to the worst part of town, where anything awful could happen . . . where something awful almost did happen?

What was I going to do the next time I saw him? I turned my face into my pillow and cried myself to sleep.

The next morning Wendy called me, demanding to know how my date went with fabulous Warren.

My mind went blank. I'd only been out of bed a few minutes and I hadn't sorted out what I was going to tell people. I had bruises on my arms and a nasty, swollen gouge in the skin over my collarbone.

I cleared my throat. "It went all right, I guess," I said, trying to sound a little bored. "Actually, Warren's not that interesting."

"What happened?" Wendy said.

"All he does is talk about himself," I said. I knew how Wendy hated that sort of thing. "Brag, brag. You know."

"Really?" she wailed. "I'm so disappointed. I was hoping he'd be terrific."

"No," I said. "And the movie was dumb. I wish I'd stayed home."

"Then you're not going out with him again?" Wendy asked.

I tried to laugh. "You've got to be kidding," I said. "I don't want to hear one more word from him about how wonderful he is. And," I added, intending to gross her out completely, "he wipes his nose on his sleeve."

It worked. "Yuck," she said. "How awful." Then she giggled. "Meg is going to die when you tell her that."

"You tell her," I said quickly. "I don't want to talk about him."

We chatted for another minute and then hung up. When I turned around, Mom was standing there, shaking her head.

"So the blond hunk from California turned out to be a jerk," she said. "I'm surprised I didn't get a phone call from you while you were still at the movie, begging to be rescued."

"I thought about it," I said. "Well, it's over and I don't want to talk about him. How's Dad?"

"Sick enough to go to the doctor this morning," she said. She poured water into the coffee maker, then turned to face me. "Are you all right?" she asked. "You look sort of shaky."

"Maybe I'm coming down with a cold, too."

"I hope not," she said fervently. "That's exactly what you don't need this close to Christmas."

I went back upstairs, thinking that a cold wasn't the only thing I didn't need. I didn't need my memories of last night, either. But I was stuck with them.

Scared again, I blinked away tears as I sprayed the scratch with antiseptic. I didn't want a scar to remind me of Warren for the rest of my life, but I was afraid I'd have one. The scratch was deep and ugly.

What would other people say if they knew he had treated me like that?

Oh, I hated Warren!

Chapter 3

Incredibly Intelligent Idea No. 3: Think of this
next time you're in class. The air you just in-
haled was exhaled by everybody else, including
the people you don't like very much.

                    Mogoo, the Mad Magician

I survived the weekend only because I came down
with a cold every bit as bad as Dad's. That gave me a
perfect excuse to stay in bed, away from the phone and
anyone who might call and want details about my date
with Warren. Mom set the small TV on my dresser and
brought me cups of hot lemonade every couple of
hours—and I made sure that the top buttons on my pa-
jamas were snugly fastened, because I didn't want to
take a chance on her seeing the ugly scratch.

My brother and sisters did me a big favor and kept
the dogs out of my room. Dad and I coughed and
wheezed for two days and then we got up and marched
off to rejoin the human race on Monday. Or at least he
did. I went to school to face Warren.

I'd hoped that he'd forget about our date and never,
never tell anybody about it. That's what I'd planned to
do. And that shows you how stupid I was. I should have
rushed off that morning ready to commit murder, but
instead I was creeping around as if I'd been the one
who'd done something wrong.

I saw Warren within five minutes after I got to school,
standing with two other boys, and all of them were

24

watching me and snickering. My face turned so red that it ached. Had he told them that poor, silly Amelia didn't know how to handle a boy who was coming on too strong, and so she leaped out of the car and ran off in the rain? Ha ha, big joke. It seemed that being a good girl meant that you might have a long walk home in your best clothes.

Before Warren had a chance to say anything to me, I whirled around and rushed off, taking refuge in the nearest girls' john. Bad move. Fritzie Seton was combing the snarls out of her ratty hair and hogging the whole mirror.

"You look awful," she said, which was more polite than she usually was to me. "Wendy's in for trouble this morning. Miss Lear doesn't like her, and cutting classes didn't help her case."

"Oh, shut up," I said. I was in no mood to be tactful.

She shrugged and grinned. "I heard that you and Warren Carey went to a movie Friday night," she said.

I glared at her and didn't answer. My comb seemed to have disappeared from my purse, no doubt dropping into that parallel universe that swallowed up odd pieces of laundry, book reports that were overdue, and all my postage stamps when I wanted to mail a letter to Heather. I pulled my fingers through my hair and it looked even worse.

"I know you asked Warren to take you out," Fritzie said.

"I did not," I said, regretting immediately that I'd fallen into the trap and was now involved in a discussion with her.

"You didn't?" Fritzie exclaimed sarcastically. "Gee, that's not what he says."

I whirled around to face her. "What?"

She put away her comb and started for the door. "You ought to do something about the way you look, Amelia," she said. The door shut behind her.

I scuttled over to one of the basins and splashed cold water on my face until I was reasonably certain that I wouldn't have a fit. Had Warren actually said something to her or was she just being repulsive again? I was certain that I would die if he told people that *I'd* asked *him* out.

I should have anticipated what was going to happen, but instead, I spent most of the morning worrying about what Fritzie said. What Warren had in store for me was a thousand times worse.

And then, of course, there was good old Miss Lear to contend with. Just the sight of that awful, skinny, hairy-legged old harpy upset me. She humiliated Wendy by refusing to let her stay in first period. "You'll have to go to the office and talk to the counselor," she said. "I can't have people wandering in and out of class on a whim. It's so terribly stressful for everyone else. You make yourself such a burden to people, Wendy."

Wendy left, looking devastated, and returned immediately, holding an admission slip signed by Mr. Depard. Miss Lear pretended that she didn't see Wendy standing by her desk and went on reading a poem she had written herself. The poem didn't make any sense, Miss Lear was too horrible to bear, and my cold returned suddenly.

I coughed until my head ached. I was sure that stupid poem was never going to end—Miss Lear had an awful lot to say about love considering that she didn't love anybody and there couldn't have been anyone who had ever loved her. The room was too hot, and I was ready to burst into tears when Wendy, standing behind Miss Lear, began mimicking her. Wendy was the best mimic I'd ever known, and that's why she was such a good clown. But this wasn't the time to demonstrate her talent.

She's lost her mind, I thought. She has a death wish.

If Miss Lear sees her, Wendy will need to move to the moon.

Miss Lear flung one arm out dramatically to emphasize a line. Wendy's arm went flying. Miss Lear lowered her voice and hunched over the sheet of paper she held. Wendy hunched over the invisible paper in her hand. Miss Lear threw back her head. Wendy's head snapped back.

I burst out laughing. I coughed and laughed, laughed and coughed. The whole horrified class laughed along with me.

"What's going on?" Miss Lear cried.

Wendy imitated her angry posture.

Everybody stopped laughing but me. I couldn't have stopped if Miss Lear had aimed a cannon at me.

Miss Lear turned and caught Wendy in the act. We're dead, I thought, but I was so sick I didn't care.

Wendy and I were sent to the office together, where she ended up talking to Mr. Depard again. I was sent home, with a warning not to come back until I was over my cold. That was the first time in my life I was glad to be sick.

After two more days in bed, I recovered completely and I trudged back to school. I told myself that no one would remember I'd ever gone out with Warren, so maybe I could face him without being overwhelmed with that awful combination of rage and fear.

But Warren had been a busy boy. Every time I passed one of his friends in the halls, the boy would stare at me. A couple of them laughed. And Warren himself made a big show of trying to avoid me, as if I actually *wanted* to talk to him.

I longed to ask Wendy if she knew what was going on, but I didn't want to arouse her curiosity if she hadn't heard anything. Meg mentioned Warren once, saying only that Wendy had told her that I'd hated our date. Mark and Carl seemed oblivious to the stares and snickers I got. But I wasn't oblivious and I needed some answers.

I got them, in the most embarrassing way possible. I'd been digging through my locker looking for a misplaced book when I heard Fritzie saying, "Oh, no. There's Amelia. You'd better hurry."

I glanced over my shoulder and saw Warren's gaze flick past me. "I wish she'd quit calling me up," he told Fritzie sincerely as he walked a little faster. "I told her she's not my type, but she can't seem to take a hint. Poor kid."

He was telling Fritzie that I'd been calling him?

I felt as if I'd turned to stone. My fists were clenched so hard that they ached.

That liar!

I turned back to my locker and blindly pawed through it. What was I looking for? I couldn't remember.

"Hey, you were home sick for a long time," someone said to me. "How are you feeling now?"

I raised my head. Curt Jerome stood over me, smiling. He wore a white sweater, and there had been a time not too long before when I would have gone slightly dizzy at the sight of him. Now I was so upset that I could barely answer him.

"I'm all right," I said. I concentrated hard on not letting tears creep into my eyes.

"You look a little wobbly," he said. "What are you poking around for? Here, I'll help you."

I remembered my library book then, and Curt pulled it out of the bottom of the pile on the floor of my locker. "This looks as bad as my locker," he said. "I'll need a stick of dynamite to clear it out."

I took the book. "Thanks," I said, trying to smile.

"Come on, I'll walk you to class," he said. "I want to talk to you anyway. You're going to the MacArthurs' New Year's Eve party, aren't you?"

"What?" I asked. "Oh. The party." I couldn't concentrate on what he was saying. My mind was filled with imagined shrieks of laughter. Warren's and Fritzie's. That monster had gotten even with me for running away from him!

We'd reached my class and I started in the door without even saying good-bye to Curt.

"Hey, are you going?" he asked.

I turned and stared at him. "Where? Oh, to the party." I felt so stupid. "I don't know yet." I slipped away from him before he could ask anything else.

I couldn't think about a New Year's Eve party! I couldn't even think about Christmas, which was practically on top of me. The only thing I was ever going to have on my mind again was that Warren Carey had tried to force me into something in a nasty old alley in the wrong part of town and now he was telling people that I had asked him out and I wouldn't quit calling him.

At lunchtime I couldn't eat. I pushed my food around in its plastic carton until it was cold. My orange juice tasted stale. My roll was so hard that I could have cracked open Warren's skull with it. I wanted to go someplace and cry.

"What's the matter?" Meg asked. "I've been watching you fool around with your food for ten minutes. Aren't you hungry?"

"I hate this junk!" I exclaimed. "Why did the school close the kitchen and start buying leftover airline food?"

Mark reached his long arm across the table and offered me a bag of potato chips. "Here, take this. You can't go all afternoon on an empty stomach."

"Do you want my lunch?" I asked.

He pretended to strangle himself. "Help. Toxic waste." He and the other kids laughed at his joke, but I couldn't.

Wendy leaned close to me and said softly, "Are you feeling sick again? Do you want me to walk to the nurse's office with you?"

"I'm not sick," I said. "I'm just bored and tired and I hate winter."

"Hey," Mark said. "Where's your Christmas spirit?"

I ignored him and got to my feet. "I'm going to my locker."

"You spend more time at your locker than anybody I know," Mark complained, but I didn't respond to that remark either.

I had to get away from them. Didn't they know that there was nothing funny in the whole world? It was only a matter of time until they heard the rumors about me that Warren had started—that I'd been the one who asked him out and now I wouldn't leave him alone. I should tell everybody what he did to me!

But who's going to believe you now, Amelia? I asked myself. No matter what you say, Warren's already covered all the bases.

I spent the rest of my lunch break tidying up my locker. The only person who stopped to speak to me was Val Guthrie, the girl I'd seen in Warren's car with him.

The girl no nice boy would be caught dead with.

"Hi, Amelia." Val's grin was too friendly. "How've you been?"

Her hair was glued into what looked like an explosion of bleached wire. She was wearing purple mascara. Her clothes weren't very clean and her perfume was so strong that it nearly made my eyes water.

I knew without a doubt that she'd heard Warren's stories—possibly from Warren himself. And now she probably thought that we were alike.

The bell rang and I muttered something—I don't know what—and ran off. I struggled through the rest of the day, unable to concentrate, hating myself for being stupid and a coward and . . . and whatever I was that had attracted Warren's attention in the first place.

Christmas was coming, but that didn't mean anything

to me. My brother and sisters were so excited that they seldom made any sense. Dutifully, I took them to the shopping mall so that they could get gifts for Mom and Dad. I helped them wrap packages. I mailed presents to my cousins, Heather in Fox Crossing and Erin in Oregon. The days dragged by and I hated school more and more. Because every day meant another triumph for Warren.

He snickered when he saw me. Sometimes he held up his hands, as if warding me off. His friends laughed and elbowed each other. And finally my friends caught on and wanted to know what was happening.

"Don't ask me," I told everybody wearily. "I think he's crazy."

One evening Curt called and asked me to drive around town with him to see all the Christmas lights. There'd been a time when I would have leaped at this opportunity. But instead I told him that I was going to do that with my family—true enough—and once was enough. Once was never enough to see the lights, but I didn't want to go. After all, who knew what Curt might try? Had he heard that I was available for parking in alleys?

Wendy and Meg told me quite sincerely that they thought I should see a doctor. Maybe I wasn't completely over my cold. Maybe something else was wrong, because I'd been acting so odd.

"I'm just tired," I said angrily. "I've got two spoiled little sisters and a brother who was probably left on our doorstep by gargoyles. I ran out of money before I could get my dad a present, so I had to borrow from Mom and she charges interest. Isn't all of that enough to make anybody 'odd'?"

They both began laughing, but then they realized that I wasn't trying to be funny. "Is there anything we can do?" Wendy asked.

I was ashamed of myself, but I couldn't apologize. Instead, I just walked away. What was wrong with me?

31

Oh, I knew, all right. I was being eaten alive by the hatred I felt for Warren. Every time I saw his tanned face (he had to be going to a tanning salon) and his smirk, I wanted to scream. No, I wanted to hurt him. I wanted to scare him as badly as he had scared me.

But he seemed so powerful. So in charge of everything. Nothing bad could ever happen to him—but lots more bad things could happen to me.

At home, we had a noisy Christmas Eve and Christmas day. I guess everyone had a good time, but by then it was impossible for me to enjoy myself, because every night I struggled through nightmares and finally I was afraid to fall asleep.

I kept going over and over that night in the alley, with Warren grabbing at me and pulling the buttons off my shirt. I kept hearing him tell me to relax.

The scratch on my chest healed over, but there was a thin, angry-looking scar left, and I was afraid Mom would see it, so I never let her catch me in my underwear.

On New Year's Eve, I phoned Meg and told her that I couldn't go to the party she and Carl were giving. I said that I had a sore throat, and I even pretended to be hoarse.

"But you've never missed one of our parties," she protested. "You've spent every New Year's Eve with us since you were eleven years old."

"I know," I said. "I'm so awfully sorry, but I can't come." And then I hung up.

I lied to my parents, too, and convinced them that I'd caught another cold. But Mom followed me upstairs to my room and put me on the spot.

"What's going on, Amelia?" she asked. "You don't look sick. Is that just an excuse so you don't have to go to the MacArthurs' party?"

I could still blush when my mother caught me in a lie. "Yes, I guess it was an excuse," I told her.

"But why don't you want to go?" she asked. She sat down on my bed and looked straight at me. "Something's happened to you and I want to know what it is."

I picked up my hairbrush and turned it over and over in my hands. "I'm tired of those parties," I said. I was unable to look at her while I talked. "It's all just kid stuff. Games and counting the seconds to midnight and kissing everybody."

"I'm sorry, but I don't believe that that's all there is to it," Mom said.

I brushed my hair slowly, bearing down hard so that the bristles hurt my scalp. "All right," I said. "It has something to do with a boy. I don't want to see him and he'll be at the party."

Another lie. Warren wouldn't be at the MacArthurs' party.

But Mom believed that, and she sighed. "I remember how hard those boy-girl things can be. But you have just as much right to be at the party as he does. Even if you've quarreled, you could still have a nice time with the other people."

I shook my head slowly. "I've already called Meg. I'd feel ridiculous calling back and telling her that I don't have a sore throat after all."

Mom sighed again. "I wish I could help you past this," she said. "Being a teenager is awful sometimes."

"Does life get any better when you're older?" I asked, really wanting to know.

Suddenly Mom laughed. "Actually, no," she said. "You just trade one set of worries for another."

I ended up laughing, too. But when she went away, I was left with myself again. I unbuttoned my shirt and looked in the mirror at my scar. Someday, somehow, I promised myself, I was going to get even with Warren.

If I had enough courage.

Chapter 4

Incredibly Intelligent Idea No. 4: Speaking for myself, I've never believed what they say happens to nearsighted teachers who eat spiders.

Mogoo, the Mad Magician

"We've invented a new character," Mark said.

"What?" I hadn't been listening to him. Outside the window of the art room, sleet blew sideways across the school lawns. January. I hated it. I hated everything.

"I said that we've invented a new character," Mark repeated. "The clowns. Remember us? We want to add at least one more to the act. She'll be called Tiny Tina, only she's going to be huge. And you'd be exactly perfect for her."

"Thanks," I said bitterly. "I've never thought of myself as huge before."

"Aw, come on. You know you aren't huge. You'd wear padding under this terrific costume. And we've got a big, frizzy, red wig." Mark pushed his drawing at me and I saw a sketch of a spectacularly funny-looking woman with bulges everywhere and hair that exploded out from under what seemed to be an aviator's cap. "See? Isn't she great? Say you'll do it. We always have fun, and we're booked solid for the next two months. Think of all the money you'd make."

I shoved the paper away. "The last thing in the world I want to be is a clown," I told him. I bent over my own drawing, trying to give him a big hint that I didn't want to talk to him anymore.

Art had always been my favorite class. Now I didn't have a favorite anything. One day dragged after another. Winter was going to last forever. And every day, every single day, I woke up knowing what I was. I was a girl the older boys snickered about.

Mrs. Nugent, strolling between tables, stopped to look at my drawing. She leaned over it, then picked it up and held it in front of her. "What are you after here, Amelia?"

I shrugged. "I don't know. It's just a landscape."

She shook her head a little, as if clearing her mind. "It's awfully dark. The trees look so—so twisted." She handed the drawing back to me and started to move on, then stopped again. "Amelia, see me after class, please." Then she walked away, quickly, as if she wanted to get away from me.

Mark pulled my drawing toward him, opened his mouth, and then shut it again. I snatched the paper away from him, crumpled it into a ball, and threw it as hard as I could into the wastepaper basket we shared.

"Why did you do that?" he asked.

"Leave me alone!" I cried.

Half the kids in class turned around on their stools to stare at me. I burst into tears and put my head down on the table.

"Amelia, step outside for a moment." Mrs. Nugent had materialized beside me, and she touched my shoulder gently. "Come on, dear. Only for a moment."

I stumbled after her into the hall, and she closed the door behind us. "What's wrong? Are you ill?" she asked.

I shook my head and wiped my eyes on a tissue, but tears welled up again.

"Then what is it? For weeks you've been—I don't know. Depressed or ill or angry. I can't tell which. Your

35

work shows it. That landscape—Amelia, that was frightening. All those crooked trees and the grasping shadows.''

"It was only a sketch," I said indignantly.

She shook her head. "Artists don't have private lives. Everything we feel shows in our work. Can't I help you? I hate to see you like this—so miserable.''

"I'm not miserable!" I protested. "Whatever gave you an idea like that?''

She shrugged then and looked away from me. "All right. I'll let it go for now. But if this continues, I'll speak to your counselor.'' She looked back at me without blinking. "Or I'll have to call your mother, because I'm truly worried about you.''

I bit my lip until the pain cleared my tears away. "Can I go back to my table now?''

She sighed and nodded, then followed me into the room.

Everybody was pretending that nothing had happened, even Mark. But a few minutes later, he suddenly whispered my name and reached out, touching my arm.

"Don't!" I cried without thinking. I flinched away from him, and my heart slammed around in my chest.

Mark turned pale. "What's wrong with you?''

I was shaking all over. Everyone was staring. Mrs. Nugent was as pale as Mark.

"You startled me," I said, and I tried hard to laugh. "I was thinking about something and you scared me.''

Mark swallowed visibly. "What were you thinking about? Murder?''

"Don't be silly," I said. But he wasn't far wrong. I'd been thinking about hitting Warren. Hitting him hard the next time he snickered at me in the hall. Hitting him so hard that he'd never laugh at me again.

What was happening to me?

The scar on my chest burned like fire. Gingerly I

pressed my hand over it, as if to soothe it. The bell rang then, releasing me from my ugly thoughts.

"I'll walk you to your next class," Mark said.

"Not unless you want to wait a long, long time outside the girls' john," I said.

"I give up," he said as he got to his feet. "Why don't you just come right out and tell me that you can't stand me?" And then he grabbed his books and walked away.

Mark had been my friend forever and we'd never really quarreled before. But he had just turned his back on me and walked off as if he hoped he'd never see me again.

I started for the door, too, wanting to get out before Wendy and Meg caught me and questioned me, but Mrs. Nugent called my name.

Now what? I thought. I stopped by her desk.

"Amelia, I meant what I said," she told me. "If I can help you, all you have to do is ask."

"You can't help," I said, and I went out into the hall.

Students streamed in both directions. Most of them were talking and laughing with friends. But Val Guthrie went slinking by alone, like a stray cat, eyeing me speculatively. I hurried in the opposite direction. Like Val, I was alone.

How many other things did she and I have in common?

I stopped in the john and looked at myself in the mirror, hating what I saw. I left again without even trying to fix my hair, which had been hanging over my eyes all day. Outside the school, the sleet turned to rain and pattered against the windows.

It had been raining hard the night I went out with Warren.

I'd been so scared, running down the dark streets in the wrong part of town.

But if I hadn't jumped out of his car, what would have happened to me? He'd torn my shirt and clawed my skin until it bled. I'd heard about things that had happened to some girls—girls you read about in the newspapers or heard about on television.

No, no. It wouldn't have gone that far. He wouldn't have hurt me that much. Things like that only happen to other people.

Don't they?

Why do I keep thinking about that night? I cried to myself. It's as if I can't control what goes on in my mind anymore. I don't want to remember! I want to be the way I was.

During lunch, I spilled juice all over the table, and when Wendy tried to help me clean it up, I yelled at her and ran out of the cafeteria. I was going crazy.

Heather had written me four times since I told her that I was going out with Warren, but I'd never answered her. I didn't know what to say. I needed to talk to her, but not through letters. And not on the phone. I needed to see my cousin, have some quiet time with her the way we did before she moved away. Heather would have understood what was happening to me. She would have known what to do.

But she had a new life now. A new and happy life, once she'd worked through the problems she ran into at Fox Crossing—that horrible housekeeper who'd tried to hurt her dog, and the mess when her stepsister was accused of something she didn't do.

I was wrong. Heather wouldn't have understood anything. She wouldn't want to hear about my problem. She'd think I was crazy, letting Warren get away with everything. Heather was a fighter, the way I'd been once.

But then, for all her problems, she'd never dealt with somebody who was always a jump ahead of her. Sometimes I wondered where Warren had learned to be so clever at anticipating what might happen next.

Could it have been experience?

Had he tried the same thing with other girls? Would he do it again?

One Saturday when I was walking through the shopping mall with my sisters, Curt caught up with us. "I hardly ever get a chance to talk to you at school," he said. "You're always running."

Cassie looked up at me. "Amelia, don't you have to go to the principal's office if you run in the halls at school?"

"Do *you?*" I asked, trying not to grin. In those days, the only ones in the world who could still make me laugh were my little sisters.

"Well," Cassie drawled, "I would if I did. But I don't, so I never do."

Curt laughed. "I hope I understood that."

Cassie scowled at him. "There's nothing wrong with the way I talk."

Curt shrugged, trying unsuccessfully to hide his big smile. "Excuse me, Miss Whitney."

He offered to buy us ice cream cones and my greedy sisters begged me to accept, so I had no choice but to follow them across the mall. While Cassie and Mimi gobbled up their treats, Curt astonished me by asking me to go to the February dance with him.

I thought I hadn't heard him right, and he had to repeat himself, adding, "I've been meaning to ask you, but you're always in such a rush."

Wendy and Meg were going to the dance, but I hadn't given it a thought. There wasn't much in the world that appealed less to me then than dancing. Or a date of any kind.

I'd already begun shaking my head when Curt said, "We ought to get a whole bunch together and go out to dinner first. Does that sound good?"

There was a time when evenings like that were such a pleasure that I hated to have them end. But now, all I could think of was the number of hours I'd have to spend in Curt's company—and what he might do if we were alone.

But we wouldn't be alone. And if I'd enjoyed dancing once, why couldn't I enjoy it again? Maybe Curt could make me happy. Once I'd thought that he might.

I nodded finally. "Okay, I'll go. Thanks for asking."

He blushed a little. "My pleasure. Well, I hope it'll be your pleasure, too."

Had he always been so awkward and bashful? Had his voice always been so, well, squeaky? Hadn't I had a mad crush on him just a few months ago?

Too much had happened to me since then.

Finally he left us alone, and I sighed with relief. There. I had a date. That ought to please Mom and Wendy and Meg. It even ought to please Mark. I was back in the land of the living. Wasn't I?

Then Monday came again, and everything that was awful turned worse. If only I had stayed home. If only I'd turned my back and run for my life when I saw Warren slouched against the wall outside the student lounge with his friends. It wasn't that I didn't have a premonition of what was coming—the moment I saw him my stomach turned over. But I'd promised to meet Wendy in the lounge and so I continued on, books clutched to my chest, eyes averted.

Warren stepped out in front of me, blocking my path. "I'm not kidding this time, Amelia," he said. "You've got to quit calling my house and hanging up when someone answers. Mom says she's going to talk to your parents if you don't stop."

His voice was loud enough to carry across the hall, and his friends stared. Warren rejoined them without looking back, and he shook his head slowly, disgustedly. "Well, what else could I do?" he asked them.

I couldn't move or talk or even swallow. I'd never called his house and hung up. I'd never called him at

40

all! Of all the people in the entire world, he was the last one I wanted to talk to, ever.

Finally I was able to unglue my feet from the floor. I moved them one after the other, heading toward the lounge. My eyes were on fire. Blood roared in my ears.

Wendy found me—I was too blind with rage to find anyone. She chattered on and on about the new clown character they'd invented, this Tiny Tina, who would distract Mogoo the Mad Magician from the zany charms of Luna Paloona, the part Wendy played.

"You see, Mogoo will go crazy over Tiny Tina," Wendy said, "and then Luna Paloona will get jealous. And then . . ."

I gawked at her. How could she be laughing about her clown act when Warren was walking around school as if he had a right to do anything he wanted to do?

"Amelia?" Wendy said. "Are you all right? You're so pale—gee. You're scaring me."

I got to my feet, shaking all over. My teeth chattered. I could feel the scar on my chest burning again.

"I'm going home," I said.

I ran for my locker, grabbed my coat, and started home. Overhead, the thick gray sky sagged with rain. Wind blew my hair into tangles. A passing car splashed mud on my clothes.

Enraged, I bent and snatched up a rock, then threw it after the car. Missed! I stamped my foot and burst into tears.

I'd never seen anyone splashed with so much mud. Wouldn't you know this would happen to me, I thought.

I wished I was dead.

Chapter 5

Incredibly Intelligent Idea No. 5: Seniors think
they're great, so don't tell them this joke. Did
you hear about the senior who stepped up to the
counter and ordered two cheeseburgers? The
man behind the counter said, "You're a senior,
right?" The guy said, "Yeah. How'd you know?"
The man said, "Easy. This is the hardware
store."

Mogoo, the Mad Magician

That night I couldn't sleep. I lay awake listening to
the furnace click on and off. Down the hall, Jamie
laughed in his dreams and the dogs ran into his room to
investigate. They must have been disappointed to find
that Jamie wasn't getting up, because they went back to
the hall and threw themselves down with thumps outside
my closed door. Probably they knew I was awake and
they were hoping that I'd go down to the kitchen and do
something interesting with food.

At three in the morning, I gave up, got out of bed,
and zipped myself into my heavy robe. With the dogs
for company, I slipped quietly downstairs, made hot
chocolate for myself, and gave each of the dogs a hand-
ful of treats. While they were still crunching, I went
back to my room and switched on my desk lamp.

I was desperate to confide in somebody, and I'd decided to try Heather. Maybe I could explain things so
that she wouldn't think I was the most stupid and cow-
ardly girl in the whole country.

"Dear Heather," I wrote. "It's the middle of the night and I think I've forgotten how to sleep."

I told her everything—how Warren had lied to me when he said that there would be other people going with us that night, and how he took me to a terrible part of town and parked in a dark alley and tore my shirt, scratched me, and hurt my arms. My hand shook when I wrote that part, so I stopped for a while, went back downstairs, and made myself another cup of chocolate. When I returned to the letter, I told her what Warren was saying about me at school.

"Sooner or later," I wrote, "my friends are going to find out that he's telling people that I've been begging him to take me out again, and calling his house and hanging up when someone answers. I'm afraid they'll believe him. Oh, Heather, I feel so bad, and there's no one I can talk to about this except you and you're too far away to help me."

I realized I was crying and wiped my eyes before tears could fall on the paper. There was no point in having Heather think that I'd come completely unglued about this.

But I had! Maybe it would be better to tell her the complete truth.

"I think sometimes that I'm going crazy," I wrote. "I daydream about hitting him and hurting him. I want to get even with him for scaring me and scratching me and lying about me. Heather, I've got a scar! And for a long time the bruises on my arms were all yellow and green and horrible. I was scared all the time that someone would see them. Warren did that to me and I want to do something back to him! I want to tell the whole world what he did.

"But he's so smart that he's always a jump ahead of me. He's thought up all those things to say that will make me look like a liar if I tell."

I had to quit writing to find another tissue. Tears just

43

kept coming and coming. Would this have happened if I'd tried to talk in person to someone about that night? Of course. I'd have sounded like a crybaby, making a huge fuss over nothing.

And that's what it was, right? Nothing. Warren hadn't really hurt me. It wasn't as if he had raped me. Not really.

I picked up the letter, intending to tear it to bits. But something stopped me. It was as if a voice spoke to me from inside myself.

Warren had taken me to a place where I didn't want to go.

Warren had held me against the seat of the car, hurting me, and he had kissed me when I didn't want to be kissed.

Warren had torn my shirt and scratched my chest.

Warren had lied about me to his friends.

He *had* hurt me!

I finished my letter and turned out my light. While I was snuggling down under my quilt, I heard Dad's alarm clock go off. Morning.

I was late getting to the breakfast table because I'd spent longer than usual trying to make myself look presentable. But my parents saw the dark circles under my eyes and commented on them as soon as I sat down.

"I'm fine," I told them. "I had trouble sleeping, that's all."

"Are you sick?" Dad asked. He'd been slicing bananas over Mimi's cereal and he stopped to look at me again.

I shook my head. "Big day today. A test and an oral report and I'm afraid it's my turn to read the bulletin in Miss Lear's class. That's enough to keep anybody awake."

"Will Miss Lear still be alive when I'm in high school?" Mimi asked Dad in a worried little voice.

"Mimi!" Mom said.

"She'll be alive and waiting for you, Mimi," Jamie said, snickering.

"She'll get *you* first," Cassie told him angrily. She poked him with half a piece of toast that had marmalade on it, and the marmalade came off on his sweater.

"Mom!" he yelled.

"Mom!" Cassie echoed.

"Amelia, please don't mention Miss Lear's name at the table again," Mom said, exasperated.

"Why am I being blamed for everything?" I yelled.

Dad looked at me without blinking. "What's going on?" he asked finally.

"Well, I say one thing and everybody picks up on it and then I'm in trouble . . ."

"That's not what I'm talking about and you know it," Dad said. "Something's bothering you and it's not the infamous Miss Lear. You've been off your feed for weeks . . ."

"I hate that expression!" I cried. "What does 'off your feed' mean, anyway?"

"It means you're acting like one of my grandfather's hens, sulking in the coop, standing on one leg with her feathers fluffed up." Dad poured himself a cup of coffee and sat down. "It means that something's happened and you can't or won't talk about it. Now this is as good a time as any to quit acting like a hen and start acting like a member of this family. What's wrong?"

I got up and started for the door.

"Amelia!" Mom called out.

But I was halfway up the stairs and I didn't answer.

What was wrong with me involved things that my little sisters shouldn't hear about, not for a long, long time.

Naturally, since I was in a terrible mood, Miss Lear singled me out for special torment during first period. I mispronounced a word while I was reading the bulletin, so she laughed. I bumped my crazy bone on the edge of my desk and flinched, so she laughed again and asked

45

me if I needed special help getting around since I was so awkward. She read another of her awful poems to the class, and that time I didn't have to suppress any laughter. I felt more like throwing up on her shoes.

Wendy asked me what was wrong as we left class, and I assured her that I was only a little tired.

"Have you been thinking about helping us out?" she asked as we threaded our way through the crowded hall.

"With what?" I asked distractedly. In the distance, I could see Warren walking in the same direction. I hoped he didn't look back and notice me.

"With Tiny Tina," Wendy said. "We'd have such fun if you worked with us. Mark's writing all these great lines for you."

I didn't answer, letting her go on and on. Finally she figured out that I wasn't crazy about this Tiny Tina idea, so she told me instead about her family's plans for skiing that weekend.

Warren was out of sight and I took a deep breath. My letter to Heather was sitting in the mailbox across from school. By noon it would be on its way to my cousin. She'd have it the next day or the day after that. What would she think? Had I been crazy to write her about Warren?

I wished suddenly and desperately that I hadn't mailed the letter, because I was absolutely certain that Heather would be disgusted with me when she read it. She'd remember Val Guthrie and wonder if I was turning into the same sort of girl. She wouldn't bother to answer me, and I couldn't blame her. And without Heather, I wouldn't have anyone left in the whole world.

During lunch, Mark plopped down in the empty chair beside me and handed me a photograph.

"This is Mrs. MacArthur wearing the Tiny Tina costume," he said. "Isn't it great? She wants you to call her as soon as you can. She said that she'll do her best to schedule you when it won't interfere with the rest of your life—I mean, she knows you help out with your sisters and Jamie and the dogs, so you couldn't always clown around with us."

I pushed the photo away without looking at it. "How many times do I have to say no to you?" I asked him. "I'm beginning to wonder if you have marbles in all your slots."

Mark's face turned red. "There's nothing wrong with me," he said, "but you act like you're not too tightly wrapped these days."

I stared straight into his eyes. "Put a sock in it," I said slowly and distinctly, and I got up and walked away with what I hoped was magnificent dignity.

I passed Val in the doorway.

"Hi," she said, smiling.

I scowled so that I wouldn't cry. But as I walked off, I wondered if maybe I shouldn't have stopped to speak to her. After all, by the time Warren was through with me, Val might be the only friend around.

Chapter 6

Incredibly Intelligent Idea No. 6: I've noticed that people don't take my excellent advice until *after* they make the mistake I was trying to warn them about.

Mogoo, the Mad Magician

At eight o'clock on Friday night, Heather called me long-distance from Fox Crossing.

I was home alone. My parents had taken the little guys to a Disney movie, and I'd turned down Wendy's invitation to go ice skating. When the phone rang, I'd just brought a plate of cookies and a soft drink into the living room, prepared to watch TV until my mind turned to mush and I stopped thinking about Warren.

"Amelia," my cousin said, "can you talk? I mean really talk, without being interrupted a thousand times by the little guys?"

"Mom and Dad took them to a movie," I said. I was close to tears of gratitude. Heather had called me instead of ignoring my stupid, whining letter.

"I'm alone, too," Heather said. "Mom and Will went to a meeting and my stepsister's at a play with her boyfriend." Heather cleared her throat, and then suddenly began crying. "Amelia, I'm so sorry about what happened to you. I can't believe anybody is rotten enough to treat you like that."

"Don't cry!" I urged her. "If you cry, then I will,

48

too, and I've already done too much of it. He's not worth it.''

"He's not worth anything!" Heather said. "I don't blame you for wanting to hit him. If I were still in Seattle, I'd hold him for you while you beat him up. Honestly! I would!''

I had a picture in my mind of Heather trying to hold Warren still long enough for me to sock him and, crazily, I was close to laughing. "I think I'd need Erin's help for that," I told her. "She's the only Whitney girl tough enough to be a physical match for him.''

"But you know that he'd never have tried anything like that on a girl like Erin," Heather said. "Jerks like him always pick on girls who have nice manners and won't punch and scream the house down.''

I couldn't help but laugh. "Remember when Erin's grandmother wrote that Erin had knocked a boy's tooth out?''

"But he wasn't trying to rape her," Heather said, and my skin prickled unpleasantly when I heard that awful word. "He'd stolen her wallet. I'll bet he didn't know who it belonged to when he took it or he'd have reconsidered.''

We both laughed, but then I heard Heather take a deep breath, and I bit my lip. Here it comes, I thought. She's going to ask me what I did to give Warren the idea he could take me to that alley.

"Amelia, you've got to tell people what happened," she said. "You're letting him get away with everything. He did something awful and you've got to tell.''

"I can't," I said. "Who would believe me now, after Warren's said all those things about me?''

"Everybody will believe you," she said. "How could you think for even a second that Aunt Ellen and Uncle Jock would doubt you? Most of the kids in your grade have known you all your life, and they'd never think that you'd make up something like this.''

"You don't know what it's been like," I protested. "If you could see how his friends grin when he's whispering to them, you'd understand what I'm up against. They believe him."

"They're seniors," Heather argued. "You don't care what they think! In a few months they'll graduate and be history."

"Fritzie Seton's not a senior and she believes him. I can tell. And I'm scared all the time that she'll tell Wendy and Meg."

"Fritzie is such an idiot that nobody is ever going to care what she thinks about anything. Amelia, listen to me. You've got to tell everybody what he did!"

I squeezed my eyes shut. "I can't. It's too late. I should have told right away. Now it would sound as if I was trying to pay him back."

"What do you care?" Heather asked sharply. "You're not thinking straight. So many people will believe you that he'll be sorry he messed with you. He'll be embarrassed and he'll leave you alone. You'll see. He won't talk about you when he finds out that you're going to fight back."

"No, it wouldn't work that way," I said. "He's so— I don't know—clever, I guess. He keeps thinking up things and I don't have a chance to do anything. I get so scared when I see him . . ."

"Has he tried anything else?" she cried quickly.

"No, no. I get scared because I remember that night, and how dark it was, and I was so far from home."

"You should have yelled until somebody called the police," Heather said.

I laughed bitterly. "In that part of town, I only would have attracted even more problems and nobody, but nobody, would have called the police for me. Trust me, I did my best to be invisible."

"It scares me even thinking about it," Heather said.

50

"Can you possibly imagine what Uncle Jock would have done if you'd told him as soon as you got home?"

I slumped in my chair. "I can imagine it now, but then all I thought was that he was so sick with a terrible cold and Mom was worried. And I was afraid that somehow he and Mom would believe that I'd done something to make it happen and they'd be mad at me."

Heather hesitated for a moment, then said, "Yes, I can see how you'd be afraid of that. I would, too. But it would have been better to tell, and it's not too late. Amelia, listen to me! Warren should be punished for what he did to you!"

"Who punishes a guy for trying to make out?" I asked angrily.

"He did a lot more than that. He took you to a terrible part of town because he thought you'd do whatever he wanted before you'd take the chance of being alone on the street there. You *know* that's what was on his tiny, diseased mind. People will want to punish him for that, I'm sure of it."

I began crying then. I couldn't help it. "No, they won't. After all, it's only my word against his, and he's made it sound as if I'm chasing after him all the time."

"Then what about all the other girls he'll try this on?" Heather asked. "Shouldn't they be warned? Shouldn't they have a choice—before they go out with him!—about whether or not they want to end up in an alley somewhere?"

I blew my nose, hard. "Thanks," I said. "As if I didn't have enough to worry about, now I have to worry about every other girl in school. Well, I *have* thought about other girls and what might happen to them. I know he's taken Val out . . ."

"Val can handle him," Heather said, interrupting me.

"Maybe," I said. "Or maybe we all like to think that she can, but she gets just as scared as we do when things go wrong."

"Then that's all the more reason why you should tell. Tell everybody for yourself, and for the other girls, and to make that guy sorry he was born! Promise me you will!"

I gripped the phone so hard that my fingers ached. "I don't know if I can."

"Well, you can tell your parents. You must!"

I blew my nose again. "I guess so. You're right. I'm just not sure how. I've waited so long and it's going to sound so dumb now."

"Meanwhile, the school's very own scum bucket is running around making other girls miserable and scared."

I groaned. "When you put it like that, what am I supposed to do?"

"Get even!" Heather shouted into my ear. "Make him sorry! Embarrass him and stop him."

One of the dogs looked in the living room door at me, wagging his tail uncertainly. My side of the conversation was bothering him as much as the other side was bothering me.

"All right," I said finally. "I'll tell my parents tonight, after the little guys are in bed."

"And tomorrow tell Wendy and Meg," Heather babbled quickly. "And Mark and Carl, because you know they'll go looking for that heap of crud and show him what being scared is really like."

"I don't want them fighting over me!" I cried.

Silence. "Oh, darn," Heather huffed. "You're probably right. But just thinking about that guy makes me want to do something awful. I mean *really* awful."

"I know," I said. "I told you, I think about hurting him all the time, and I end up hating myself for enjoying the idea."

By the end of the call, I promised my cousin at least a dozen times that during the weekend I'd tell everybody I knew what Warren had done to me. She hung up and

I admitted to myself that I did feel better, now that I'd planned to do something to help myself. I even deluded myself into thinking that maybe I'd be happy again after I'd put the blame for that night on Warren instead of dragging it around myself.

Heather was absolutely right to give me the advice she did. But neither of us understood what was in store for me.

I'd barely settled myself down on the couch in front of the TV before the phone rang again.

Heather again? No, it was Curt Jerome.

"This is a surprise," I blurted. "I thought you always worked in your uncle's store on Friday nights."

"I traded with my cousin because he wanted tomorrow night off," he said. "When I drove past the ice rink, I saw Wendy and the rest of your gang going in. If you'd been with them, I'd have gone in myself. How come you're home? Do you want to go skating? I'll pick you up if you do."

I was tempted to go—really tempted—because then I wouldn't be able to tell my parents about Warren that night, and maybe the whole thing would go away before morning and I wouldn't have to think about it again, ever.

What's more, here was Curt, the boy I'd had such a big crush on, wanting to take me out.

Two reasons to go.

But Warren was out there somewhere, doing his thing, hurting people, then laughing and lying about it afterward.

"I can't go, Curt," I said, "but thanks for thinking of me. I'm waiting for my parents to come home. Important family business."

"Well, gee," he said slowly, sounding puzzled, "can't it wait until you get back? Or if they're already in bed, couldn't you talk about whatever it is in the morning?"

"Nope," I said, trying to sound cheerful, as if this family meeting wasn't going to be a horror story. "I'd sure like a rain check, though."

"I have to work next Friday for sure," he said, "but how about next Saturday? No, that's the night of the dance." He laughed. "I wouldn't forget that."

"That's good," I said.

"Well, at least we'll be going out next weekend," he said. "Maybe we'll get some skating in another time."

"Sure," I said.

I could tell Curt about that night, right now while he was on the phone. I could get it over with before the dance.

"Well, guess I'll get going," he said vaguely.

No, I couldn't tell him. It wasn't possible. I'd sound like a whiner, a crybaby. Oh, boo hoo, that big awful boy made a pass at me and scared me. I'm just a little girl and I need my mommy and daddy.

"See you, Curt," I said, and I hung up, fast, before I changed my mind.

I sat in front of the TV again, staring blindly at the screen. Oh, Heather, I thought, I wish you were here with me. I'm really scared of what people are going to think of me.

I can't do it.

But somewhere that night, Warren might be smiling and lying and making plans, and another girl could end up running home in the dark.

Or maybe she won't have the chance to run.

I heard my father's key in the front door lock and I pressed my fingers against my lips. Here I go, I thought.

Chapter 7

Incredibly Intelligent Idea No. 7: I told Luna Pa
loona that my head felt stuffed up, and she said
she was surprised, because it looked empty to
her.

Mogoo, the Mad Magician

Mimi and Cassie were too tired for snacks, but Jamie
wanted hot chocolate and a sandwich before he went to
bed, and so I sat in the kitchen with him and my parents
for what seemed like hours.

While my brother told and retold the movie plot to
me, I told and retold a different—and horrible—tale to
myself. I planned exactly how to tell my parents about
Warren. There was no point in taking forever with it,
but I wanted them to know how scared I'd been—and
how humiliated I was now, since Warren had begun
spreading his lies. But at the same time, I was worried
that I might give them the idea that I'd led Warren on,
making him think that what he'd started out to do was
all right with me.

"You're not listening to me, Amelia," Jamie said.

He startled me and I jumped a little. "Sorry," I said.
"I really did hear you."

Jamie opened his mouth to argue, but Dad broke in.
"I don't think we've got time for a pop quiz on the
movie, Jamie. Finish your sandwich and head upstairs
for bed."

Jamie went, reluctantly. There was a long moment of

55

silence while my parents looked at me and I looked at the floor.

"Have you decided to tell us what's bothering you?" Mom asked quietly.

I nodded. Now that the moment was here, my tongue had stuck to the roof of my mouth.

Dad stood up abruptly. "I'm still hungry. Let's fix a proper late-evening snack. We need a real meal for a real discussion." He opened the refrigerator and began pulling out everything in sight. "Ellen," he said to Mom, "we're going to need one of your special salad dressings—don't forget the olives. Amelia, you chop up the peppers for the steaks and slice the bread. We'll talk as we work."

Tears stung my eyes—Dad had known how to make this easier for me. We could work and not look at each other.

I had finished my story just as Dad took the steaks out from under the broiler. Mom set the salad on the table, and we all sat down.

"Did he hurt you?" Dad asked. He raised his gaze and looked straight into my eyes.

"The bruises on my arms are gone," I said, "but . . ." I opened the top buttons of my shirt and showed my parents the thin, pink scar. "He scratched me."

Then I saw that Mom's lower lip was shaking.

"Oh, Mom, don't cry," I begged. "It didn't hurt. Not much, anyway. Not as much as my arms. And it's all over now."

She shook her head. "I'm not going to cry. I'm angry because I can't grab him right this minute and smash his head against the wall." She cut a huge bite of steak and crammed it in her mouth.

Dad took a piece of bread from the plate. "I know that you told us as soon as you could talk about it, but I wish . . ."

"I know," I said.

56

"We would have called the police," he said.

I gasped. I'd never thought of involving the police, of actually telling officers what had happened. Or if I'd thought of it, I'd pushed the idea away instantly. They'd want to know what I was doing in that part of town, in an alley. They'd ask why I'd gone out with someone like Warren in the first place.

"No, I couldn't have told the police," I said.

"But he's going unpunished," Dad said. "Oh, yes, I could go to his house and talk to him and his family. I'll still do that—I'd like to make him sorry he ever met you—but . . ."

"No!" I cried. "Don't do anything. Don't you understand what's happened? He's told people that I chase after him, ask him out, call his house and hang up when someone answers. His family would think I've lied to you about him."

"We know, but we can't let that stop us," Dad said.

I pressed both hands to my eyes. "Please," I begged. "Let's not even think about talking to his family or calling the police. It's too late, anyway." I picked up my knife and fork then, and tried to cut my steak. "Please," I begged again, "can't we just eat and talk and let this whole thing go away? Otherwise, I'll wish I hadn't told you anything."

My parents and I ate our late meal in silence, and then, when we'd finished, Dad said, "We have to do something. *I* have to do something."

"Anything we do now might only make things worse for Amelia," Mom told him. "I can see the bind this boy's put her in. No matter what she says, he's got the perfect answer."

"And he's been saying these things about you at school?" Dad asked.

"Well, to his friends," I said. "The senior boys, at least. A few others, I guess. I don't know how far it's gone, but none of my friends have said anything."

57

"Would they?" Mom asked.

I shrugged. "I think so. I think they'd want me to know what he's been claiming. I'm scared all the time that they're going to hear the rumors."

"They won't believe him," Mom said.

"Do you think they will, Amelia?" Dad asked.

I shrugged again. "No. Well, I hope not. That's why I decided that I'd better tell them the whole thing, including how he's been making fun of me whenever he sees me alone. Sorta beat him to the punch, if you see what I mean."

"You should have done that before," Dad said.

"Dad," I said, pleading.

"She's done the best she could," Mom told him.

"I know." Dad was clenching and unclenching his hands. "I can't stand this. I don't know myself how I'm going to handle it, so I don't have a right to tell you that you've been right or wrong. But after this, please, don't shut us out. If anything like this ever happens again . . ."

"Oh, Jock," Mom cried.

"It's not going to happen to me again," I said. "I learned more than I ever wanted to know about being cautious."

We had a big family hug then, stacked the dishes in the sink, and turned out the kitchen light. On the way upstairs, Mom asked, "When are you going to tell your friends?"

"Tomorrow morning," I said. "The clowns are working in the afternoon, but if I go over to Wendy's right after breakfast, I can tell her then, and I'll try to catch Meg before lunch."

"Maybe they'll tell the others for you," Mom said, sounding hopeful. "If they start rumors in the opposite direction, Warren might learn a useful lesson himself."

"That's what I'm hoping," I said.

But later, while I was staring wide-eyed into the dark,

I felt quite certain that Warren wasn't going to learn anything from me, not the way I was going to fight back. I was like someone standing in front of a firing squad, saying, "Please, let me tell you the way it *really* happened."

I was about to fall asleep when Mimi and both of the dogs crept into my room.

"Amelia," Mimi whispered, "can we get in bed with you?"

"All of you?" I asked, rising up on one elbow. "Do I have to have all three of you?"

The dogs leaped nimbly up on the bed, answering their part of the question. Mimi hoisted one leg over the edge of the mattress and patted my shoulder.

"We'll try not to take up all the room," she assured me.

"You already did," I said. "What's the problem, kids?" Mimi and the dogs had crawled into bed with me before, more times than I could count, because of bad dreams (hers or theirs—I was never certain), loud noises outside, guilty consciences (collective), or too many bedtime snacks.

"Well," Mimi began, making herself comfortable under my quilt and preparing to make a mini-series out of her story, "if I don't like kindergarten—and I think I don't—then am I going to like first grade? You see, Amelia, in kindergarten they don't let you go to the bathroom when you need to go but only when the rules say you can. If you can't go when you want to go, then you aren't able to go when they say you can go."

I understood her problem exactly. "Didn't Mom tell you what to do at times like that?"

"No. Did she? Did I forget?"

"I bet she told you," I said patiently. I was at a point where I'd rather worry about her problems than my own. "She told us all. Whenever an adult does something to you—or says something—that really and truly could hurt

59

you, then you just go do what you know is right, and if they get mad, you tell them to call Mom or Dad for clarification of the issue.''

"What's clarification of the issue?" Mimi asked.

"That means that Mom or Dad will tell them that you don't have to stay in your seat when you need to go to the bathroom, just because your staying in class is convenient for your teacher or anybody else in school. Understand? You don't do anything that can hurt you or embarrass you because somebody tells you to. Not even a teacher. Always, always remember that if anybody tries to make you do what's wrong, tell them to call Mom or Dad right now, because if they don't, you will.''

"For clarification of the issue," Mimi repeated solemnly.

"Right.''

"I'll remember," Mimi said.

I wished that I had. Wouldn't Warren have had something interesting to think about if I'd told him that I could only go into that alley if my family had said it was all right, so I was just going to nip on home and ask them first?

The dogs were asleep and snoring, and Mimi drifted off a few minutes later. There was no room for me in the bed, so I tiptoed down the hall to her room and crawled under her blankets.

"Amelia?" Cassie asked from the next bed.

"Yes," I groaned. Now what?

"Did you tell Mimi to go to the bathroom whenever she really and truly had to go?"

"Yes," I said.

"I told her that a million, zillion times!"

"She needed somebody big to tell her."

"Oh.''

I, Amelia Whitney, was too old to expect other people to tell me what to do, but since I couldn't seem to make sensible choices by myself, I felt like an idiot because I'd needed Heather and my parents to point out the obvious to me.

I also, at that particular moment, hated growing up!

Chapter 8

Incredibly Intelligent Idea No. 8: People who write on bathroom walls are stupid, crude, and boring. They also have rotten handwriting—I have an awful time reading their stuff.

Mogoo, the Mad Magician

I called Wendy after breakfast and told her I was dropping by her house around ten, but before I arrived, the clown troupe showed up at the Ingrams' unexpectedly. When I got there, I could see Mark, in his Mogoo clothes, through the living room windows.

Disappointed, I rang the doorbell—and a huge woman in a frizzy red wig answered.

"Wendy?" I asked suspiciously. Ordinarily, she was Luna Paloona, the weird vamp wearing a slinky dress but with half her teeth blacked out, and I wasn't exactly certain if she was now the character in the wild, biker-woman outfit or if a stranger was in the costume.

"Who else?" she groaned, patting the padded dress that hid her cute little shape. "Mark wanted to rehearse with Tiny Tina, even though you won't play her and we can't find anybody else we like enough to spend all that time with. We're sort of a family, and not everybody fits in, you know." She adjusted her plastic nose. "Really, Amelia, you ought to feel sorry for me. I'm not the type for Tiny Tina, and you'd do her exactly right."

I slipped past her bulk. "What ever gave you an idea like that?" I complained. "I tried Drama for one semester at school, and every time I stepped out on stage I nearly died of fright. You guys are the actors.''

"But you're so . . . so sassy!" Wendy said, following me into the family room. "You always were the one with the quick wit."

Mark, dressed as Mogoo, turned around when I came in. "Ah, there you are. I heard what Wendy said—you'd really be perfect for Tina. You and Heather could always crack everybody up without even trying."

"Heather moved away and I feel about as funny as a broken arm," I grouched.

This clown conference caught me off guard. I'd been rehearsing what I was going to say to Wendy, but there was no way I could tell her about Warren with Mark and Carl listening.

"Well, excuse me for breathing," Mark said, whipping off his top hat and bowing to me. But he was grinning. At least, Mogoo was grinning.

I sighed and looked around. Carl, who was ridiculous Officer Maquick, the policeman who always arrested the wrong person, now had a bright red patch on the seat of his baggy trousers. It looked as if he'd sewn it on himself. Meg, dressed as Beano the Bum, was fastening a huge, rusty safety pin to her ragged overcoat. "Look at this great pin, Amelia," she said. "I found it on top of the neighbor's garbage."

"Yuck," I said

I must have sounded actually disgusted, because Meg looked up at me and I caught a glimpse of her hurt expression under the makeup.

"I wasn't exactly digging through it," she said. "I was just walking by . . ."

"Sorry," I said, but I didn't have the energy to sound very sincere. I wandered across the room and sat down by the big window. Outside, Wendy's dog and cat sat together on the deck, watching a grumpy seagull perched on the garage roof.

"Well," Mark said uncertainly, "maybe we could go through the act once more and give it a try this afternoon."

"No way," Wendy said. "I just can't do it. Tina's funny, but there's no way I'll ever be able to pull off that tough, wisecracking way of hers."

"Amelia, you could try on the costume and get the feel of it," Carl said. "Then, maybe, you'd do a little horsing around with us . . ."

"How many ways can I say no?" I asked.

Inside, I was ready to scream. How could they possibly think I'd ever been sassy enough—self-confident enough—to play the part of terrible Tiny Tina, a clown with a really wicked sense of humor? They were talking to Amelia, the coward who'd run away from Warren instead of punching him out, the timid little mouse who was afraid of passing him in the halls at school.

They gave up, and while they made their plans for the afternoon, I watched the seagull glowering down at the dog and cat. He finally made them nervous enough so that they scooted inside through the dog door. Satisfied, he flapped away, heading west toward Puget Sound. The world was full of bullies.

The clowns finished their business, took off their costumes, and, except for Wendy, left. Wendy stuffed Tiny Tina's clothes into a garment bag and sat down next to me.

"My folks went shopping, so we're all by ourselves," she said. "You want to tell me now what's going on?"

I blinked. Had everybody known I was keeping a secret?

"I'll tell you, but you've got to promise not to say anything until I'm done, and then please, please don't tell me what I should have done. I can't stand being reminded of what a coward I am."

Wendy nodded soberly and pulled the cat to her lap,

hugging it, as if she was a little scared and needed comfort.

I told her the whole thing, but I couldn't look at her. Instead I looked at the dog, who was lying on his back, asleep.

When I finished, Wendy made a strange, half-strangled sound. I looked up at her and saw that she was blinking hard. "I'm going to kill him," she said. "I really am. He makes me sick! I wanted to do something awful to him two weeks ago when he asked me to tell you to quit calling him up."

"What!" I cried.

"He told me—I was walking with Meg and Carl—he told me that you were calling him up every night—or calling his house—and then hanging up."

I clenched my fists so hard that my nails cut into my palms. "Did Meg and Carl hear?" I asked.

"Sure. He wanted them to hear. I told him he wasn't lucky enough to have you call him up—ever. I said he was probably being called up by people he owed money to."

"Thanks," I said. I slumped in my seat. "Thanks for sticking up for me."

"Didn't you even suspect that he was lying to people besides the senior boys?" Wendy asked.

I shook my head. "Just Fritzie, and you know how she is. If there's any gossip floating around, it sticks to her like lint, whether she was supposed to know about it or not. I must be really dumb. Seniors always think the rest of us don't matter, so I figured that he wouldn't bother lying to sophomores."

"Trust me, he bothered," Wendy said quietly.

I covered my face with my hands. "How many people think I've been calling him?"

"Nobody!" Wendy cried. "Well, hardly anybody. Most of the kids think he's been calling you."

I rubbed my eyes hard so they wouldn't fill with tears. "Why didn't anybody tell me?"

"Because we knew your feelings would be hurt," Wendy said.

"Does Mark know?"

Wendy shrugged. "I don't honestly know. We haven't all been sitting around gossiping about you, if that's what you're afraid of. If Mark heard about it, he hasn't said anything. But then, he wouldn't. He'd die before he'd do anything to hurt you."

I realized that I was wringing my hands and quit. "Then all this time you've known . . ."

"Not the whole time!" Wendy said. "And we certainly didn't know what he did to you, only what he's been saying about you—that you've got a crush on him and won't leave him alone. Like I said, nobody's believing that stuff."

"Nobody's going to believe what he did to me, you mean," I said.

"Of course they will!" she insisted. "We'll tell everybody and you'll see. They'll gang up on Warren. Mark will knock the hump off his nose."

"Warren doesn't have a hump on his nose," I said.

"He will after Carl puts one there."

Suddenly both of us were laughing and crying at the same time. She hugged me and I hugged her, and we swore that we'd make Warren sorry for what he'd done.

She made me feel so good. Except for my cousin Heather, Wendy had been my best friend all my life. Why hadn't I trusted her to believe me and care about me?

She fixed lunch for us, and persuaded me to go along with the clowns to watch their act. They were doing a show at a mall south of Seattle, and as long as I was only going to be a spectator, I was glad to go.

We rode in Mrs. MacArthur's van, and everybody tactfully avoided bringing up Tiny Tina, although her costume was hanging on the rack in back. When we got to the mall, the kids pulled on their clown clothes while they were still in the van, scrambling over each other and bickering about wigs and noses. Mogoo's hat had a new dent in it, which Mark blamed me for, and I grabbed the hat away from him.

With my thumb, I dented the other side of the hat. "Now you've got stereo," I said, handing it back.

He looked straight into my eyes and for a second, neither of us said anything.

"Help me with my makeup," he said finally, grinning a little. If I hadn't known him better, I would have sworn that he was blushing, too.

"Let her help me!" Meg said. "I've got all these clothes to put on and it takes forever. You're practically ready to go, Mark."

"I'll help Meg," I said. Suddenly, strangely, I didn't want to be that close to Mark.

I'd helped out with makeup before, so I knew what to do. Just for fun, I gave Beano more pointed eyebrows than he usually had, and everybody pronounced them absolutely perfect.

They like me, I thought, even though some of them might really believe I've been calling Warren.

I felt appreciated for the first time in weeks, and while I trailed along behind them after they left the van, I thought that maybe someday—maybe!—I just might try on that Tiny Tina outfit. I could draw a tattoo on my arm—no, don't be tempted. It would be better if I stayed a spectator.

But Mark wouldn't let me. Halfway through the clown act, Mark, as Mogoo, strutted to the edge of the platform and looked down where I was standing.

"Hey, there, beautiful girl in the red jacket," he said to me. The crowd became very quiet, watching and waiting.

Mark knelt. "Pretty girl," he crooned. "I see you. Come up here and give me a kiss."

I shook my head.

"Pretty girl," he singsonged, "you come with me and I'll make you my magician's assistant. I'll saw you in half and then all three of us will go out on the town. Dining, dancing, you name it. Come on, honey. Don't be scared. Mogoo will take real good care of you. Just relax."

I panicked. My heart slammed into my throat. I couldn't talk or even breathe.

Relax. That's what Warren had said to me.

Was the crowd laughing? I couldn't tell, because there was a roaring in my ears. I pushed away, shoving people aside, and when I broke free, I ran.

But the memories of that night ran with me, whispering to me, flashing pictures in my mind, pictures not just of what had happened, but of what might have happened if I hadn't been able to escape.

Oh, why couldn't I be like Mimi again, with my biggest worry whether or not I'd be excused from class to go to the john?

What went wrong that I was now pursued by this fear that the world was out of control and dangerous, and something, somebody, was always coming downhill at me and I couldn't get out of the way?

Chapter 9

Incredibly Intelligent Idea No. 9: Don't dance
holding an open umbrella. It annoys everyone.
                        Mogoo, the Mad Magician

I had no way of getting home. I didn't even have
money for a phone call. The mall was at least fifteen
miles from my neighborhood, and I couldn't think what
to do.

My heart beat too fast and I was soaked with cold
perspiration. All around me, people rushed this way and
that, pushing, shoving, glaring angrily at everybody else.
I found myself at the opposite end of the mall from the
place where the clowns were performing, but I needed
to get even farther away.

I'd humiliated myself in front of my friends and several hundred strangers. They all thought I was crazy,
and they were right. I'd ruined the show for the clowns.
There was no way Mark could have covered up my
panic. He was quick-witted and funny, but I'd made fools
of both of us. He'd never forgive me.

And neither would Meg and Carl, even if Wendy explained to them what had happened. Although their
mother wasn't making money from the performance—it
didn't have anything to do with her catering business—
she'd still set everything up for them. What I'd done had
made her look stupid, too.

But I couldn't have stayed there, letting Mogoo the

Mad Magician come on to me like that. Reaching for me. Saying he wanted to kiss me. Telling me to relax.

Oh, I hated that expression now. I never, ever again wanted to hear anybody tell me to *relax*.

What was I going to do? How could I get home?

I saw a mall security guard talking to an admiring group of little kids. I could ask him. . . .

I really was crazy. Go up and tell the security guard that I needed to go home because I was scared and I didn't have money to call my mommy?

Now I was too hot. The mall was blistering, and I had to get outside where I could breathe. I walked toward the doors, yanking off my coat.

Rain poured in the parking lot. I put my coat back on and walked, walked, up one row of cars and down the other. People stared at me. Well, why not? How often did they see a lunatic girl stomping up and down, crying?

"Looking for your car, babe?" A guy with too many big white teeth and pale blond hair blocked my path.

"What?" I asked. I'd frozen in place.

"Looking for your car?" he repeated. "Need a little help?"

He didn't want to help me. He wanted something—I didn't know what—but I had to get away from him. I whipped around and ran in the opposite direction, darting between cars, too afraid to even look back and see if he was following me. I was alone again, in a place where I didn't want to be, and I was too old to be so scared.

I returned to the mall, with the jumbled idea that if he was following me, I could find one of the security guards and turn him in. Yes, that's what I'd do. I'd say, "This guy is following me and . . ."

And what?

People glanced uneasily at me as I rushed past. I saw their expressions and resented them until I recognized myself in one of the mall mirrors. *I* was that wild thing with wet hair and gray skin, whose clothes were drenched—dripping!—and whose eyes streamed with tears.

"Hey! Quit running!"

Carl, dressed as Officer Maquick, grabbed both of my shoulders.

"Stop it! Stop it right now!" he commanded.

For an instant, I couldn't breathe. Then I threw my arms around him and sobbed. "Oh, Carl, a guy was following me and I didn't know where to go or how to get home, and . . ."

"Hush," he whispered against my neck. "It's okay now. I've got you safe, and nobody's going to hurt you. We won't let 'em. The clowns are going to take care of you and make everything turn out right." He rocked me back and forth, as if I'd been Mimi or Cassie. "Amelia, Wendy told us what Warren did. We ended the show and couldn't find you, and she thought Mark had scared you off, so she told us what happened to you. Mark's so sorry. He's looking outside for you. Don't cry anymore, because we're going to fix everything. Wait and see."

Mrs. MacArthur found us then. She looked flushed and upset, and I thought she was angry with me. But she cleared that up right away.

"Amelia, Wendy told us why you were so frightened. If I could afford to hire a hit man, you can be sure I'd be setting up interviews right now." She brushed uselessly at the water streaming from my clothes. "We've got to get you into dry clothes."

"Here comes Meg," Carl said. "She can take Amelia into the john and let her change into the Beano costume."

Silently, Meg wound her arms around my neck. Behind her, Wendy grinned a little. Her Luna Paloona vamp makeup was smeared, as if she'd been crying.

"You scared us, pal," she said mildly.

71

"Sorry," I said. "I feel like such an idiot."

"Panic attack," Mrs. MacArthur said, nodding her head briskly. "Tell me about 'em. All I need to go into a Class-A panic attack is a distant view of a wasp."

"Yeah," Carl said. "Once Mom was stung about a hundred times and nearly died . . ."

"And now just the sight of one makes me crazy." She pried Meg loose from me and pointed the two of us toward the restrooms. "Meg, help Amelia out of those wet clothes and let her wear Beano's clothes going home."

The moment Meg and I were inside the restroom, I started bawling all over again, scaring two elderly ladies half out of their wits. Or rather, I thought I was the one scaring them.

"She'll be okay," Meg told them.

"Who are *you?*" one of the ladies demanded of Meg.

"I'm a girl!" Meg cried quickly. "This is a costume." She'd caught on to their problem faster than I.

They left, glad to get away from us, and Meg leaned against the wall, laughing. "That happens all the time," she said. "Whenever I'm dressed up like Beano and need to use a public john, I wonder if that's the time I'll be arrested for starting a riot."

She peeled off the baggy costume she wore over her own clothes and handed it to me. "Now I really look weird," she said, "but I'm not going to take time to get all this makeup off now. I'll do it in the van."

I changed in a booth, and came out with my wet clothes rolled in a wad. "Wonderful," I groaned when I saw myself in the mirror.

"Let's get going before anyone else comes in," Meg said. "Together we look so ridiculous that we're likely to give somebody a heart attack."

"I'm sure making a lot of trouble for everybody," I said as we shoved open the door.

She nudged me. "You're not the one who caused the

trouble," she said. "Don't get that idea. Somebody else is the cause, and boy, is Mark mad. No kidding, Amelia, he and Carl are going to make Warren wish he'd never met you."

I grabbed her hand. "No, they can't do anything," I said. "It would only make everything worse. I'm so sick of the whole thing, and I couldn't bear to see them get in trouble because of me."

Meg looked at me in astonishment. "Warren needs to be dragged behind a car for ten miles! Or dropped out of a plane. He'll be lucky if all they do is tell him off."

"Please!" I pleaded. "Help me talk them out of it."

She shook her head. "Nope. I'm going to help them. I'm going to egg that creep's car Monday, toilet-paper it Tuesday, write "pig" on his windshield in lipstick on Wednesday, tie Luna Paloona's underdrawers to his antenna Thursday . . ."

I couldn't help but snicker at that last idea. Luna Paloona's drawers were long, striped in red and black, and decorated with the most hideous green lace I'd ever seen.

"See?" Meg said, giggling. "This situation is going to offer us a million opportunities."

We were both laughing when we joined the others. Mark was there, too, knocking rain off his top hat. "You okay?" he asked me.

I nodded. I'd talk to him later about junking his plans to get even with Warren for me.

We ran to the van through the cold rain. The kids still in costume peeled them off quickly and stuffed them in their garment bags, then fastened their seatbelts and passed around paper towels and a fat jar of cold cream.

"Ready?" Mrs. MacArthur called out.

For some reason, Mark looked at me at that moment. "All set?" he asked.

"Let's go home," I said quietly.

73

Mom was in the kitchen when I walked in, still in Beano's clothes, with my own under my arm.

Her face went white. "What happened?" she cried.

"Nothing, nothing!" I responded hastily. "I got caught in the rain and my own clothes were dripping, so Mrs. MacArthur suggested I wear Meg's costume."

Mom turned back to the vegetables she was stir-frying, but I saw that her hands were trembling a little. "Aw, Mom," I said. "Don't worry so much. I was with my friends."

"I know," she said, and she laughed shakily. "I can't imagine Carl or Mark ever . . ."

"Never," I said firmly. "I'm going upstairs to change clothes, but I'll be right back down to help with dinner."

Mimi and Cassie clattered in and stared at me. "What are you doing in Meg's clothes?" Cassie demanded indignantly. "You don't look anything like Beano. Where's your big red nose? Where's your hat with the umbrella on top?"

I explained again how I came to be in Meg's costume, but the little guys were as indignant as they would have been if I'd stolen the clothes. They followed me upstairs, along with the dogs, to continue their complaints.

We passed Dad in the hall. "Well, Amelia, I see you've decided to dress for success," he said, trying not to grin. "It's a big improvement."

The little guys giggled, but they still followed me. "Are you going to be in the clown act?" Mimi asked. "Are you? Can you? Will they let you?"

I shook my head firmly. "No, never."

The next day, Sunday, was quiet and rainy, and my friends each called me twice during the day to see how I was getting along. I appreciated the attention, and worked hard convincing the boys that they couldn't do

74

what they wanted to do most—beat the stuffing out of Warren.

Mark was hardest to persuade.

"You can't imagine how much I want to do something to him that hurts," I said, "but that's me. You weren't involved and I'd die if you got in trouble because of me."

"But . . ." he began.

"Please don't make things harder for me," I begged. "I've got all the worry I can handle now."

"Every time I even think of him, my brain feels like it's boiling," he said.

"I know. But please promise you won't make things worse for me."

He didn't say anything for a second, and then he sighed. "I promise. I know you're right."

But I was still uneasy. The next day at school, we were all going to talk openly about my date with Warren, and I admitted—to myself—that I was afraid of what the result might be.

I was right to be afraid, but the disaster came sooner than I expected.

Chapter 10

Incredibly Intelligent Idea No. 10: My friend told
me that all my great ideas bring tears to her eyes.
But once she told me the same thing about her
report card.

Mogoo, the Mad Magician

The next morning I put on the clothes that made me
feel my most self-confident—the great sweater and skirt
Mom gave me for Christmas—and my favorite boots.
My hair looked perfect for a change, and (this will be
hard to believe) my fingernails were my own and all
were the very same length. With that much going for
me, you'd think that I'd go off to school in such a powerful mood that I'd be ready to take on a dragon and
Miss Lear at the same time. Warren, look out, I thought.

Wendy, Meg, and I had a quick chat after we met at
school, and while I dawdled on my way to class, they
did as we'd planned and told my secret to three of the
girls who were also stuck with Miss Lear for homeroom.

Mark dropped into my room seconds before the last
bell rang, to ask me how I felt and tell me that I looked
better than just good. To my astonishment, he hugged
me, too, and then sauntered away while Miss Lear sent
him a long, poisonous look.

The bell rang. Miss Lear was still looking at me. So
were the three girls who'd just learned what Warren had
done to me.

Suddenly I wished I'd stayed home.

"Amelia, read the bulletin," Miss Lear said.

I got up and marched forward.

Fritzie Seton whispered, "There's dog hair on your skirt, Amelia. But I guess you don't care. All the boys want to take you out now, no matter what you look like."

Half the class heard her and laughed. The other half gawked, wondering what was funny.

I stared down at the bulletin, but the print blurred so much that I couldn't read it. I shoved it back into Miss Lear's hands.

"Why do we have to read these stupid things?" I cried. "We hear most of this garbage over the loudspeaker."

"Take your seat," Miss Lear said. "And don't think I'm going to forget your bad attitude. Fritzie will read the bulletin."

I headed toward my place, hoping I wouldn't trip over my feet and fall flat. As soon as I sat down, Brad Willis, the boy behind me, leaned over my shoulder and whispered, "Good for you."

I was too panicked to look around and see if anyone else approved. Fritzie read the bulletin, drawling each word as if it had special meaning, and when she was done, Brad clapped and yelled, "Not bad for a graduate of the Bride of Dracula Charm School!"

"To the office, Brad," Miss Lear said, her voice flat and mean.

Brad got up and shuffled off cheerfully. I glanced quickly at Meg, for she'd had a halfway crush on him since Christmas, and saw that she was grinning in admiration.

Suddenly something was happening in the class. I couldn't have explained it, but a sort of electricity was passing between the kids. There was a lot of whispering, and I heard my name more than once.

"Class!" Miss Lear said sharply. "Settle down."

People were turning to look at me. Was it because I was rude to Miss Lear? Or because of Warren?

I dug out my homework and put it on my desk, pretending that I wanted to look it over. My face stung as if it had been slapped. I could feel eyes staring at me. Even after the whispering died down, I knew everybody was thinking about me.

Maybe laughing at me.

I was the subject of gossip now, for one reason or another. Did it matter why? I was miserable.

Miss Lear finally got control of the class again, but I couldn't concentrate on anything except my embarrassment. Don't think that I was ever Miss Perfect around school. That's not true. There were times when my cousin Heather and I got into a lot of mischief. But it was always the funny kind—practical jokes and silly pranks. Neither one of us had ever been *whispered* about.

By lunch break, all the sophomores knew what had happened to me, not only in first period but also the night I was stupid enough to go out with Warren. When I walked in the cafeteria, kids stopped talking to look at me.

"Nice going," one girl said. "I'd have given six months' allowance to have seen you tell off that old witch Lear."

I grinned with gratitude and scooted past her to my place at the table where Wendy, Meg, and I usually sat. I'd barely settled down when Fritzie bent over me.

"Don't you just wish that Warren had made a move on you," she said, and she laughed.

"Oops!" Meg cried as her orange juice splattered in an arc, across Fritzie's hair and face. "Sorry. It slipped right out of my hand. How utterly and completely awful, Fritzie. Can you ever forgive me?"

"You did that on purpose!" Fritzie yelled. "Look at this mess!" She yanked tissues out of her pocket and

78

dabbed at her face and hair, making everything a thousand times worse because bits of tissue stuck to the juice in her hair. A fuzzy wad of it was plastered to her forehead. The harder she tried, the worse she looked, and finally someone took pity on her and told her that she'd have to use water to wash off the sticky juice, because she was beginning to look like a character from a horror movie.

She rushed off, and Wendy, Meg, and I looked soberly at each other.

"If she says one more word about Warren, I'll help her get that tissue off with sandpaper," Meg said.

I shook my head. "Thanks, but you'd better stay out of this. I don't care what she says. She's never liked me anyway, and I always did think she could win a Biggest Jerk in School contest."

"No, that goes to Warren," Wendy said. "Have you seen him this morning?"

I pushed my sandwich away without tasting it. "From a distance. He didn't see me."

"You look like you're scared of him," Meg said. "Quit that. He's the one who ought to be afraid of you now."

I shrugged. "It doesn't seem to work out that way. He was the one who did something wrong and I'm the one who keeps getting hurt."

"That's going to change," Wendy said. But she was mistaken.

Before my last class, Warren caught up with me in the hall. I sensed that someone was walking beside me, but I was searching through my stuff for the pencil I seemed to have lost, and so when I finally did look up, I was too startled to speak.

He was smiling a cold, plastic smile. "I heard your version of our date," he said. "That was a great story. Just about the funniest one I ever heard."

"Get away from me," I said, but I was so scared that my voice shook.

"Not yet," he said, and he leaned his head close to mine. "I want you to get something straight. Your little joke was funny for a while, but if you keep telling lies about me, you'll find out what real trouble is."

"Lies!" I cried. "You're the one who's the liar."

He stared at me, as if he was astonished. "Quit it, Amelia. Quit lying and phoning me and following me around. I don't want you. Is that clear enough?" Before I could answer, he whirled around and took off in the opposite direction.

I stopped in my tracks. Was he crazy? He looked and sounded as if he believed his own lies.

He *was* crazy.

And scary.

When I got home from school, I found the house empty except for the dogs, and a note from Mom on the refrigerator explaining that she and the little guys were grocery shopping and would I please fold the laundry for her. I'd barely started when the phone rang.

I hoped it would be Wendy. I'd already told her what Warren had said to me in the hall, and I figured that by now she'd have thought up a way to make me laugh about it.

But it was Curt Jerome calling. He sounded odd, as if he was calling a stranger. "Amelia?" he asked. "Is this Amelia?"

"Of course it is," I said. I couldn't help but laugh.

"I didn't recognize your voice," he said huffily.

"Sorry," I said quickly. "What's new, Curt?"

"I just got home," he said. "Mark and Carl and I were talking after school."

My stomach felt as if there was a rock in it. I couldn't think of anything to say.

But that was all right, because Curt didn't wait for me to say anything. "They told me about that date you had

80

with Warren Carey," he said. "I never did understand why you wanted to go out with him in the first place."

"Well . . ." I began.

"And then when they told me that you let him take you to . . ."

"I didn't *let* him take me anywhere!" I cried. "Well, I agreed to go to the movie, but . . ."

"I mean, Amelia, what did you do to make him think that he could . . ."

I had spots in front of my eyes and my ears were ringing. "Curt, listen to me, I didn't do anything! He just, well, he took everything for granted. He was horrible! He hurt me and scared me so bad that I have nightmares."

"I'd heard something about you and Warren," he said, going on as if I hadn't spoken. "I was going to ask you about it, but things kept coming up. I guess I didn't want to get into it."

"What did you hear?" I asked numbly. As if I didn't know.

"That you call him and follow him. That you want to go out with him again, but he thinks you come on too strong and want to go steady and all that."

"He only says that so people won't believe me."

There was a short and very awkward silence. "Well, maybe," he said. "But that wasn't the real reason I called. It looks like probably I won't be able to go to the dance Saturday, because, uh, well, my car's got something wrong with it and I can't use Dad's car because my mom is sick and might have to go to the doctor. She's really sick, I think, and so probably I can't take you to the dance. This is sort of an emergency."

"But the dance is just days away," I said without thinking, because I had just gone brain dead. "Maybe your mom will be better then."

"No, I don't think so," he said, sounding even more

vague than before. "It doesn't look like I can make it. Now I gotta go, because somebody's at the door."

And he hung up.

I went upstairs and sat on the edge of my bed for a long time.

Chapter 11

Incredibly Intelligent Idea No. 11: I told Luna Paloona that our relationship seemed to be hopeless. She said she never thought it had been even that good.

        Mogoo, the Mad Magician

The next morning at school, I told Wendy and Meg that I didn't have a date for the dance—and why.

Wendy shoved her jacket in her locker and slammed the door so hard I expected it to fall off. "Curt is a weasel," she said, and she kicked her locker for emphasis. "His mother isn't sick. And his car works just fine. He drove it to school this morning."

"Why would he say that?" Meg asked. "Is he going to the dance with somebody else?"

"Maybe," I said. "But I think it's because of Warren. He said I shouldn't have gone out with him in the first place, and he asked me what I did that made Warren think . . ."

"He what?" yelled Wendy. "He wanted to know what *you* did?"

"Since when is it the girl's fault when a guy starts acting like he just got out of the loony bin?" Meg complained.

Far down the hall, I saw Val Guthrie hurrying along, alone as usual. A new and very uncomfortable idea struck me.

"You're saying those things because you know me,"

I said slowly, thinking hard. "But what if you'd heard the same thing about Val?"

My friends eyed me suspiciously. "Well, Val," Wendy said disgustedly. "She'll go out with anybody."

"But what if you'd heard the same thing about her?" I persisted. "That she'd had to go home alone, at night and in the rain, because a boy wouldn't let up on her."

"We'd say that she'd brought it on herself," Meg said quietly. She paused. "Maybe she hadn't done anything. Maybe she'd only gone out with the boy because she thought he really liked her."

"And he didn't," Wendy continued for her. "He was only out for what he could get."

The three of us were silent for a long moment. Then Wendy said, "I'm just as bad as everybody else. Somebody ought to take out my brain and scrub it clean with a wire brush."

"Yeah," Meg said. "My brain won't take very long because I think it shrank up to pea-size the last time I passed along a nasty rumor about Val."

I sighed. "Guess I can't blame Curt for breaking our date then. In his place, I might have done the same thing."

"But he knows you!" Wendy protested.

"He didn't want to be seen with me," I said. "That's what it comes down to in the end."

After that, I saw Curt as often as I ever did, but he never again said so much as hi to me.

The following days were the most painful of my whole life. Even remembering them now hurts me. I'd thought that everybody would support me. Well, everybody except Warren himself, his thick-necked macho buddies, and Fritzie. But that's not what happened.

At first I was the invisible girl at school. I could tell who had heard about Warren and me by the expressions on their faces as they passed me in the hall and tried to pretend that I wasn't there.

Next I became an embarrassment. Some of the girls looked so uncomfortable that I felt sorry for them. A few of the boys snickered, but many flushed and looked miserable when my gaze met theirs.

And then something strange happened. I'd ducked into the girls' john to comb my hair, and Franny, a girl I barely knew, suddenly began crying.

We were alone, and my automatic response was to ask her if I could help her.

"No," she said. "I heard about what happened to you. I'm so sorry. It was really awful and somebody's got to do something about that guy." She wiped her eyes on a paper towel and looked everywhere but at me. "Of course, I can't *exactly* understand how you feel—I mean, nothing like that has happened to me, you know. I've been very careful. Nothing like that ever could happen to me—and nothing worse ever happened to me, either."

I was so astonished at her outburst that I couldn't think of anything to say.

"I mean," Franny went on desperately, "I've heard about things like that—everybody has—so I decided that I wouldn't go out with boys anymore."

I nodded. "Maybe you're right."

She opened her mouth to say something else, and then, without even a good-bye, she ran for the door. I was left feeling certain that something horrible had happened to her, sometime, someplace. Poor Franny. How many other girls were keeping secrets like that?

Brad Willis caught up with me outside the library one afternoon, red-faced and awkward. "Amelia, do you remember my sister, Joanna?"

"Sure," I said. "She's away at college now."

"Once . . ." he began. His nice face contorted into a terrible scowl. "Once a guy drove her to another town and pushed her out of the car because she wouldn't do what he wanted."

"Oh, Brad, I'm so sorry," I said quickly.

"But I got even," he said, lowering his voice. "I'll do it for you, too, if you want. I told Meg and she said to ask you first."

"What did you do?" I asked, fascinated and horrified at the same time.

"A couple of us guys got him and drove him to the same town and shoved him out."

There was a meanness in me in those days, in spite of how hard I tried to keep it down. So I said, "That wasn't bad enough. A guy doesn't have as much to worry about after dark as a girl."

Brad grinned wryly. "We thought about that. So we took his pants and his shoes before we pushed him out of the car."

My meanness got the better of me and I burst out laughing. The idea of Warren walking home from somewhere without his shoes and pants cracked me up completely.

"I'll do it to Warren if you want me to," Brad said earnestly. "I know a lot of guys who'd help."

I shook my head. "No. Thanks, but I don't want you to get into trouble. That's a funny trick, but it must be against the law or something."

"What Warren did to you is against the law, Amelia," he said.

I grabbed his hand and squeezed it. "I just want girls to know about him so they don't make the mistake about him that I did. I'll be satisfied if he doesn't hurt anybody else."

We went our separate ways then, and I was silly enough to believe what I was saying. I actually thought that my story could warn girls off Warren. Incredibly, nothing seemed to make a difference. I often saw girls walking with him in the halls—and he always made a point of slipping his arm around their shoulders so I could see. School gossip reported that he had dated the homecoming queen, then the junior class president, both in one week. Wasn't anybody taking me seriously?

Meanwhile, at home, my parents were having a hard time with all this, too. Dad still wanted to call the police, even though he realized that no one would believe me after all that time. Mom decided that she was going to tell Warren's mother that her son needed help from a psychiatrist, but Warren's parents were in Hawaii and the cleaning woman who answered their phone said she neither knew nor cared when they were coming back, and she wouldn't take a message because she hated the job and was quitting anyway.

Wendy and Meg phoned me every night, even though they saw me every day, and Mark began calling me, too, but he seemed to be as interested in repeating his new clown jokes as fretting over me.

"Listen to this," he said one evening on the phone. "Mogoo comes up to Luna Paloona and says, 'If you come back to me, I'll give you a ring.' Then he puts this ring on her finger—it's got a glass doorknob on it instead of a diamond. So Luna looks at it and says, 'If I die with something like this on my hand, will you please remove it before notifying my next of kin? I'd hate to have them see me like this.' "

I was eating an apple when he called, so I still had my mouth full and was chewing thoughtfully. "I don't know if that's funny or not," I told him. "I'd have to see the ring first."

"I'll bring it over," he said. "I found it in that junk shop where we found the necklace that Luna wears, the one with the plastic teeth and glass rubies."

I wasn't exactly in the mood to look at a ring made out of a doorknob, but my homework was finished and I didn't have anything else to do. "Okay, come on over," I said. "But I don't want to hear one single word about Tiny Tina."

"Not so much as a syllable," Mark said.

He was there in ten minutes, holding out the silliest ring I'd ever seen. My dad happened to wander through the front hall about then, and he saw the ring, too.

"Good grief," he said to Mark. "If that's all you can come up with for an engagement ring, don't bother asking me for Amelia's hand in marriage." Dad and Mark had always joked around together.

Mark looked down at the ring in mock dismay. "But I spent a dollar and a half on it," he wailed.

Dad, on his way toward the kitchen, called back, "Wait until you can afford five bucks, or forget it."

Mark grinned at me. "Seriously, now, what do you think of the ring?"

"It's really awful," I told him sincerely, "and it's going to get laughs all by itself, even if you don't think up anything funnier for Luna to say."

"Help me out, then," he said. "We're afraid that we're getting in a rut. We've got this birthday party Sunday, and we did the act for the same little girl last year. We need new stuff."

"You do lots of different acts," I said. "Can't you switch bits and pieces around?"

"Recycled old stuff is still old stuff," Mark complained. He settled himself down in the living room, with a dog on each side of him. "Help me think."

It took a while, but ideas began coming. "You could have Luna change her mind about Mogoo and start chasing him," I said.

"We thought of that, but it wouldn't work unless we had you-know-who in the act, too, so Mogoo could fall for her and make Luna jealous." Mark smiled innocently at me.

"Okay, scratch that idea," I said quickly. "Try this. It's been ages since Officer Maquick arrested Luna for anything. He could catch her with this ring and accuse her of stealing it."

88

"Yes!" Mark said. "Good. And then Mogoo can deny giving it to her, just to pay her back."

We went on and on, sketching out a whole new skit. Mark called the other clowns and they hurried over. Together, they worked out the act, and for that whole delicious evening, I forgot all about Warren and school.

I got through the week and made it to Saturday by telling myself that everybody was going to forget about me soon, remembering nothing except that Warren wasn't safe to date. Saturday, the day of the dance, was going to be a hard one to handle, so I made plans to take the little guys ice skating in the afternoon, hoping to tire myself out so much that I'd be able to fall asleep by eight that night. However, before the kids and I got out of the house, Meg phoned.

"I hope you're sitting down," she said. "I've got a shock for you."

"I'm not sitting, but go ahead," I said. Mimi and Cassie were watching me suspiciously from the hall door. What now? their expressions asked.

"Wendy slipped on their sidewalk and broke her leg."

"What?" I exclaimed.

Meg repeated herself. "It happened this morning. She's in the hospital and won't get out for a week. Then she'll be in a cast for a million years, her mom said."

"But is she going to be all right?" I asked.

"Sure, sooner or later. But right now she can't have visitors except for her family, so Carl is going crazy and sending bushels of flowers and tons of candy. Mrs. Ingram said she's been trying to call you for hours but there wasn't any answer."

"We've been shopping all morning, and I was just leaving to take the kids skating. But maybe I'll go to the hospital instead." I was ignoring the looks Mimi and Cassie were giving me.

"There's no point," Meg said. "You can't see her until tomorrow."

"Then I'll be first in line," I said.

"We're going to have to cancel out on that birthday party," Meg said. "With only three clowns, the act will be awful."

"No, it won't," I said. "You'll do fine. Wendy would want you to at least try."

"She'd want you to help out," Meg said quickly, as if she was out of breath.

"Aw, quit that," I said. "You know I don't have that kind of courage. I'd make an idiot out of myself."

"That's the whole point—making an idiot out of yourself," Meg said. "And you get to hide behind all that makeup and the costume. If I couldn't hide, I couldn't do it. I feel like a different person once I'm in Beano's clothes. I *am* different. Completely free to do anything I like. It's really wonderful, Amelia. You ought to try it just once."

She'd said something that caught my attention. "I feel like a different person."

I wouldn't have to be Amelia Whitney for a couple of hours. Tiny Tina, the big, ferocious woman with the tattoo, who rode motorcycles and wore an aviator's leather cap, would have taken Warren apart and put him back together backward if he'd tried anything with her.

Tiny Tina could take care of herself. She wouldn't care what anybody said about her.

"I'll do it," I said.

Meg screamed so loud that she nearly broke my eardrums. "I'll be over in ten seconds with the guys and the costumes," she said. "We'll work out everything before—uh . . ."

"Before the dance," I said. "I know you're going with Brad."

"Okay. We'll work it out, then," she said. "Don't move. We'll be there instantly."

When I hung up, the little guys were glaring. "You aren't going to take us, are you?" Cassie asked.

"I can't," I said. "I'm going to be a clown instead. You always wanted me to be a clown, so don't you want to stay and watch me practice?"

Cassie and Mimi exchanged one of their mysterious looks.

"Okay," they said in unison.

"You can take us skating some other time—soon," Cassie added.

A few minutes later the doorbell rang and Cassie let in Meg, Carl, and Mark. Mark handed me a garment bag. "Tina," he said, "you are the woman for me."

He was laughing, but his eyes were sober and kind, and he seemed different to me. Not just a friend. Something else. Maybe he was someone I could trust.

Look out, I told myself. Like Franny, you have to be very careful now.

Chapter 12

Incredibly Intelligent Idea No. 12: Luna Paloona
said she didn't want to date anyone who kept a
rabbit in his hat, since it got loose in restaurants
and went after the salad bars. You get girls like
that sometimes. I guess you just have to write
them off as too picky to please.

Mogoo, the Mad Magician

I slept late Sunday morning even though I'd gone to
bed at eight the night before. I was hardly awake when
my cousin Heather called me from Fox Crossing.

"I can't stand it anymore," she said. "Have you told?
What's been happening? Why didn't you call or write?"

"Sorry," I said. "Yes, I told, and it's all over school
now. I didn't write because I've been waiting for something to happen—I don't know what. I thought that everybody would jump in and support me. You know, run
Warren out of town or throw him in the Sound off the
back of a ferry. But most people pretend that I'm invisible. It's as if I'm the most embarrassing thing to happen
around school since the beginning of time."

"And Warren? What's happening to him?"

"Nothing," I said. I repeated Brad's offer of revenge
and Heather laughed.

"Sounds right to me," she said. "But are you telling
me that people are still speaking to him?"

"Sure," I said bitterly. "Except for my friends. Actually, some people I thought were my friends seem to be having more trouble looking at me than they do him."

"Don't start feeling like you're the one who's the monster," Heather said.

"I'm not!" I said.

"You sound like you do," she argued.

I chewed my lip reflectively. "Okay. I guess I do sound like that. I feel like that. But it's hard not to." I told her that Curt had broken our date and why. "See?" I concluded. "What's not my fault ends up being my fault anyway."

"Boys should not be allowed," Heather said angrily.

"Allowed to do what?" I asked.

"They shouldn't be allowed to *be!*"

I couldn't help but laugh. "I know you don't mean that. At least as far as your boyfriend is concerned."

"You're right. But I get so mad thinking about what happened to you."

"Ha. You're not the only one. We're all having our bad moments around here. If I could do it all over . . ."

"Stop that! You don't have to do anything over. Warren's the one who needs to go back to square one."

"He won't," I said. "Listen, enough about me and my troubles. You'll never believe what happened to Wendy yesterday. She slipped on the ice and broke her leg."

"Is it bad?" Heather asked quickly.

"Her mother said not too bad, but she has to stay in the hospital for a few days, and then she'll have a cast and crutches and all that. I'm going to see her first thing this afternoon. Compared to her, I don't have anything to complain about."

"Poor Wendy. I'll write her a letter and send her a book of those weird cartoons she likes so much. But you, you do too have something to complain about. Amelia, promise you'll stop putting yourself down."

I yanked my hair in frustration. "Am I doing that?"

"You said that compared to Wendy you didn't have anything to complain about. *Yes, you do.* What happened to you matters a lot, and don't you forget it. You've got a right to feel bad and be angry."

"Sure," I said, but I didn't believe her. Not totally. Bit by bit my right to be me was being worn away.

After we hung up, I ate breakfast with my family, then went back to my room to try on Tiny Tina's costume. For a long time I studied myself in my mirror. I could feel myself changing, becoming strong and sassy. Carefully, I applied Tina's makeup and pulled on her huge, frizzy wig. Better and better, I thought, as I yanked the leather aviator's cap over the wig. Then I stuck on the red plastic nose and twirled around in front of the mirror.

Perfect. I wasn't Amelia Whitney anymore. I loved the feeling.

When Meg and I got to the hospital that afternoon, we found Mark and Brad there ahead of us. Wendy's room was full of flowers and balloons, and although she was groggy and half-asleep, she was glad to see us.

"I heard the news," she told me. "You're going to do Tiny Tina."

I looked at my watch. "In exactly one hour and fifty minutes, I'll be ruining your act."

"You will not," she said. "Mark told me that you're wonderful."

"And when you get out of here, we can have a great time playing both your characters against Mogoo," Mark said. "Carl's got dozens of ideas for that."

I held up my hand in protest. "I didn't say I was going to do this forever. I'll help only until Wendy can be Luna again."

"Sure," Meg said hastily. "No problem." But I wasn't sure she was sincere. I had a vague suspicion that

I was being led firmly into a career as a clown, whether I wanted it or not.

Well, I told myself, as Meg said—no problem. For the time being I was more than willing to be Tiny Tina. I needed to escape from Amelia and all her unsolvable troubles.

We didn't stay at the hospital long, because Wendy kept falling asleep while we were talking to her. And we had things to do to get ready for the party.

At the last minute, I almost changed my mind. We were at the MacArthurs', getting into our costumes, when I suddenly realized what I was doing.

"You feel nervous because you don't have your makeup on yet," Meg said. "As soon as you look in the mirror and see Tina, you'll be fine."

She was right. By the time we crawled into the van, I was so completely Tina that when Mark tried to help me, I doubled up my fist and socked his arm so hard that he yelped.

"I don't need help," I told him as I settled myself down in a seat.

"Someday you'll change your mind," he said, as he tried to twirl Mogoo's long, black cape and succeeded only in tangling it around Meg's head.

"Everybody buckled up?" Mrs. MacArthur called from the driver's seat.

"Let's go for it!" Carl yelled, and off we went.

The clowns always put their costumes and makeup on before they arrived at parties. Little kids got such a kick out of seeing a van-load of clowns pull up in their driveways. And we began our act as soon as the van doors opened.

Mogoo hopped out, twirled his cloak, and offered his hand to me. I slapped it aside and leaped out, my padded costume bouncing around me. I could see a dozen pairs of eyes watching from the house windows, but I pretended that I didn't.

Officer Maquick pretended to threaten Beano with his club and Beano ran for the front door. Someone inside opened it, and Beano, with Officer Maquick in hot pursuit, ran inside. Meanwhile, Mogoo the Mad Magician pulled paper flowers out of his sleeve and offered them to me. I turned my head away and marched toward the door. Mogoo followed, offering me a plush rabbit from his hat and a plastic parrot that he pretended to pull out of my wig. I turned on him and swatted him with the huge, plaid purse I carried. The little kids were screaming with laughter.

I didn't need to wait until the end of the party to know that I was a success.

The clowns were booked to play at a school for handicapped children Tuesday morning, which meant that I had to arrange ahead of time to be excused from my morning classes. On Monday, I told myself that I wasn't going to have trouble with Miss Lear, the way Wendy always did, because I was going to outsmart her. I wouldn't ask her to sign my permission slip before or during first period—I'd wait until all the other teachers had signed, and then slip in just as lunch break was ending and stand beside her desk until she came in, hand her the slip, and wait until she wrote her name on the only blank line left.

But my plan fell through. Everybody in the office was busy, and I didn't get my slip until after second bell rang, which made me late to first period, so I needed an admission slip for that, too. Bad start.

Fritzie was taking roll when I came in. I handed my admission slip to Miss Lear and was going to take my seat when she stopped me.

"What's that other slip you're carrying?" she asked. Oh, no. "It's a permission slip for tomorrow," I said. "Why?"

I explained that I was going to the special school with the clown act.

"What for?"

I explained that I was the new clown.

Miss Lear took the slip between her thumb and fore-finger and placed it on her desk. "I'll look at it later," she said.

"It'll only take a second to sign it now," I babbled. I couldn't let that slip disappear into the bottomless pit where Wendy's always went.

Miss Lear fixed her mean little eyes on me. "I'll think about it later," she said.

"But . . ."

She moved away from her desk, heading toward Frit-zie, holding out her hand for the attendance sheet.

Everyone was staring at me. What would Tiny Tina do?

I stood right where I was, and when Miss Lear wandered back, she pretended surprise. "You still here?"

"I'll wait while you sign the slip," I said firmly.

Her eyes grew bright. "You like being the center of attention, don't you? I'm afraid melodrama won't solve your situation in this class."

"What?" I gasped.

She smiled and looked down at the attendance sheet, as if it were a fascinating secret document. "You'll find that your sad little stories won't get you special favors here. You seem to generate stress wherever you go, Amelia. Well, I don't have time for all that neurotic nonsense. Now take your seat."

"What are you talking about?" I whispered frantically.

But she was no longer listening. She began speaking to the class as if I wasn't there. Fritzie was ecstatic, but Meg looked ready to cry.

I took my seat, burning with anger and embarrassment. No one glanced at me. I was invisible again.

I knew what Miss Lear meant by "sad little stories." She'd heard about Warren, and she didn't believe me.

But the class wasn't over and Miss Lear had more in store for me. For homework the week before, we had turned in outlines for short stories that we were going to write that week. The stack of outlines sat on Miss Lear's desk, and she picked them up and sorted through them.

Then she looked at me. "I'm surprised by this outline, Amelia," she said, smirking. "I thought you'd have a much more exciting tale to tell than this one."

Fritzie laughed aloud.

Miss Lear went on, commenting on first one outline and then another, but I couldn't understand anything she said. My mind was buzzing and my stomach churned.

I hated her! I hated her ten times worse than I had before. And there was absolutely nothing I could do about it.

When class was over, I picked up my unsigned slip and took it to the next class, where it was signed promptly. But by that time I was too upset to be grateful.

When was this mess with Warren going to end? I was tired of being a victim over and over again.

I went to the special school the next morning with the rest of the clowns, even though I knew I'd be in trouble because of Miss Lear. So as soon as we returned to our own school, I went straight to see my counselor, Mr. Depard.

He interrupted me before I finished explaining my unexcused absence and my problem with Miss Lear. "You're having the same trouble Wendy has," he said, sighing so that I'd know what a pain I was. "You can't expect Miss Lear to take the responsibility for your activities outside of school. Actually, you're fortunate that you've been allowed to take part in this . . . this clown business."

"Wendy always makes up the work she missed, and I will, too," I said.

"That's not really the point, is it?" he said. "We

have to have rules. You can't expect to go on breaking them forever, now can you?''

"I wasn't expecting that.''

He fiddled with a pencil, then with a folder on his desk. I waited. He sighed.

"I've been meaning to speak to you about something else, Amelia,'' he said finally. "I just hadn't found time yet.''

You haven't found time to tie your shoe again, either, I thought, looking down at the shoelace straggling on the carpet.

"I had a very upsetting conversation about you,'' he said.

I looked up at him in surprise. "About me?''

He nodded and leaned back in his chair. "Ordinarily what happens outside of school would not be our responsibility,'' he said.

I waited.

"But you've made certain charges around school, upset students, disrupted the routine . . .''

"What are you talking about?'' I asked. My mouth was dry and I needed a drink of water but I was afraid to ask.

Another big sigh. "This business with Warren Carey,'' Mr. Depard said. "His parents are out of town, and he's new here. He went to the senior class counselor for advice, and Mrs. Carpenter spoke to me about the problem.'' Mr. Depard looked straight at me. "You're causing him considerable embarrassment, Amelia. Perhaps it never occurred to you that a young man could be terribly hurt and bewildered by an attack against him such as the one you've launched.''

He hadn't asked me to sit down but I did, because my knees didn't seem to be strong enough to hold me upright anymore. "Attack,'' I repeated. "I didn't attack him. What did he tell you?''

Mr. Depard held both of his hands palms up, as if to

say that the answer should be obvious. "Why, he didn't tell me anything directly. I told you that. But Mrs. Carpenter said that Warren felt you were spreading malicious gossip about him in retaliation for what you perceived as his rejection of you. His grades are in jeopardy—his parents have ambitious plans for his education. He's been embarrassed in front of his friends. Now it seems to me that you and he should be able to work all this out. If you apologize, no more will be said about it, I'm sure."

"But he's the one who's been lying about me," I cried.

Mr. Depard looked at me. "Perhaps the two of you have very different ways of seeing the situation," he said.

I gritted my teeth. "He tried to—to attack me. Or is tearing my shirt and bruising my arms and scratching my chest only a 'different way of looking at the situation'?"

Mr. Depard's face turned bright red. "If that's true, why didn't your parents call the police?"

I got to my feet. "Because I was stupid and didn't tell them right away. I was afraid and humiliated, and I wanted to forget the whole thing." I stomped to the door and turned to look back at him. "Now I wish I'd kept my mouth shut forever, because the way things are going, I'm going to end up being blamed for everything from Warren's hurt feelings to air pollution and the national debt." I slammed the door as hard as I could when I walked out.

Mrs. Camp, the secretary, ran after me as I stormed through the office, and grabbed my arm just as I pushed out the door.

"Amelia, wait," she whispered. "I couldn't help but hear. Listen to me. If you need someone to talk to, go see the nurse. She's better at handling things like this than anyone else."

I looked at her silently and pulled my arm free.

"Please," she whispered. "Don't think that everybody has the same attitude. I've heard about what happened, too. It's an outrage. Talk to Mrs. Larson. She can help."

"She helps liars?" I asked angrily.

Mrs. Camp flushed. "No, Amelia," she said. "She helps women like us. You and me. You're not the only one who's fought this battle. Some have fought ones that were even worse."

Tears stung my eyes. "I feel so stupid," I said. "Every time I see him, I want to run away or hit him or scream. And now I find out he's been telling his counselor his lies. And my counselor doesn't believe me."

Mrs. Camp patted my arm. "It's hard for men to believe. Or rather, it's hard for them to admit that they believe, because if they do, they have to act. Be committed. Put themselves on the line for what's right."

"Not even women want to do that," I said.

"Some won't," she said, and she laughed a little. "Cowards support the people who look the strongest, regardless of right or wrong."

I promised I'd think about seeing the nurse, and I went to class. But I couldn't concentrate on anything except Warren, Warren, Warren.

What would Tiny Tina do about all this?

Chapter 13

Incredibly Intelligent Idea No. 13: I don't bother discussing my report card with my parents anymore. They never have anything new to say about it.

Mogoo, the Mad Magician

When I got home after school, I found Mimi and Cassie dancing and yelling in the kitchen and my mother bent over the counter, laughing hysterically.

Jamie, wearing an expression of patient endurance, swallowed a mouthful of peanut butter sandwich and said, "Mimi had a fight with her teacher."

"What happened?" I asked Mimi. But she, still dancing and shouting with laughter, was beyond answering.

"Somebody tell me!" I demanded.

Cassie pushed her glasses on straight. "Mimi needed to go to the bathroom and her teacher wouldn't let her leave the room."

"Oh, no, not that again," I said.

Mom straightened up and wiped her eyes on a paper towel. "Wait till you find out what she did."

"Do I want to hear this?" I asked warily.

"Sure," Jamie said. "Mimi's famous now."

"What did you do?" I asked Mimi, grabbing her as she danced past.

"I went to the principal and told him that my teacher wouldn't let me go to the bathroom so I was going to call the police." Mimi nodded emphatically. "And maybe the president, too."

"What happened?" I asked. I hadn't had a very successful day with figures of authority and I couldn't help worrying about my baby sister.

"He wrote me a note," she said, and she dug a folded piece of paper out of her pocket. "Here. Read what it says. I forget some of the words."

"She doesn't know *any* of them," Jamie observed.

I read the note aloud. "Be it known that Ms. Mimi Whitney has my permission to go to the restroom at her own discretion." I looked up admiringly. "Gee, Mimi, that's better than he ever did for me when I was in your school."

"What did he do for you?" Cassie asked.

"He told me not to bother him and take care of the matter myself."

Mom laughed again. "I think he's getting tired of dealing with assertive Whitney women."

"Good," I said. "I hope everybody feels that way."

"But," Mom said warningly, looking at each of us in turn, "I don't want you to get the idea that I'm encouraging you to sass your teachers and do stupid things at school. Your cousin Erin ought to be a lesson for you— her grandparents wrote me that she's been suspended again and I'm afraid she deserved it. I want you to stick up for yourselves if you're really and truly being treated unfairly, and not just because you don't like being told what to do."

Wait until you hear my story, I thought. You're going to think that the Whitney women bring out the worst in everybody. Poor Erin probably didn't get a chance to tell her side of the story.

That night after dinner, I told my parents what had happened that day. My father's reaction was exactly what I'd expected.

"I'll see Depard tomorrow," he said, "and we'll get a few things straightened out."

The day before I would have begged him not to make a fuss, but Tiny Tina had taken me over, some time between my talk with the school secretary and the time I got home and heard about my little sister's courageous stand.

"Go ahead," I said. "It's all right with me. I think it's about time that he found out there are people who are on my side."

"You mean the kids at school still aren't sticking up for you?" Mom demanded.

"Are you kidding?" I asked. "Every day things get worse. Mrs. Camp in the office told me that people—men especially—don't want to believe that women can get into serious trouble without deliberately bringing it on, because if these people believe it, they're afraid they'll be obligated to help stop it. I guess nobody really wants to get involved with anybody else's problems."

Dad shook his head sadly. "I'm sorry to say that she's right. Just about everyone's been guilty of looking the other way at one time or another."

"I'm going to school with you tomorrow," Mom told Dad. "And I'm going to ask that the principal sit in with us while we talk about this. They've known Amelia for a year and a half. If they can't judge what sort of girl she is by this time, then they'd better learn to pay more attention to what's going on in the school."

"Mr. Depard knows what I'm like," I said bitterly. "It was just easier and less complicated to believe Warren's story."

"Well," Dad said, "let's see if we can make the easy way out a little more painful for everybody who tried it."

For a quick moment, the old Amelia crept back, about to protest the fuss that was coming. But Tina stood up inside me and said, "Good. If I can't get any other satisfaction, at least I want to make Warren sorry he ever met me.'' And I shook my fists the way Tiny Tina did.

Things started out with a big bang the next morning in homeroom. Miss Lear asked me for proof that I'd had an excused absence the day before, and I whipped out the slip Mrs. Camp had given me.

"Of course," I added sweetly, smiling a Miss Lear smile, "this is only a formality, since you already knew where I was." I pretended a great big sigh. "Paperwork, paperwork. Such a bore."

The class was very quiet, waiting to see what Miss Lear would do.

She didn't do anything. She didn't even take the slip out of my hand, but instead she pretended that I was invisible. That was just dandy with me, so I strutted over to Fritzie and handed the slip to her. "For your collection," I whispered.

Halfway through class, Miss Lear sent me to the office to pick up copies of something she'd forgotten. This was a task she usually gave the student she was the most annoyed with at the time, but this was the first time she'd ever selected me. In the office, Mrs. Camp asked me if I was still interested in talking to the nurse.

"She's in her office every day after school for a while," Miss Camp said. "I know she'd be glad to listen."

I shrugged. "I guess I could drop by." I wasn't terribly enthusiastic, but it sounded like something that could help. Even Tiny Tina might need advice now and then, although, of course, there was no guarantee that she'd take it.

I carried the stack of papers back to Miss Lear, who took them from me without thanking me. She never thanked anybody. Amelia's feelings would have been hurt. Tina had Miss Lear's number and didn't bother getting upset over the small stuff.

Occasionally I thought of my parents, who were coming to school sometime during the day, and each time I felt a little uneasy until I remembered that my family had a right to be heard and a right to defend me to anybody at any time.

But when Meg skidded into the cafeteria, late for lunch, to tell me that Mom and Dad had just marched into the principal's office with Mr. Depard trailing behind and wringing his hands, I could feel the blood drain from my face. Panic hit me full force.

"Oh, boy, I think I'm in real trouble now," I groaned. I'd told Meg my parents were coming, but now that the moment was here, all the awful possibilities I could imagine occurred to me at once.

Meg nudged my arm. "Quit it. You won't be in trouble, but Warren will, and so will Mr. Depard."

I calmed down, remembered Tina, and stuck out my chin. "We'll block 'em, shock 'em, and knock 'em," I said in Tina's voice.

Meg cracked up. "I can't get over how you took to playing our new clown. Sometimes I think you're changing to be just like her."

"Gee, I hope I don't start looking like her," I said.

"No chance. Not as long as you only eat half of your food." Meg reached for the dessert I'd just pushed away. "Do you care if I take this? I'm still hungry."

"Try this, too," Brad said, sitting down next to her and dropping a chocolate bar in front of her. He looked at me, then, and his smile faded. "How's everything with you, Amelia?"

"Fine. Mostly fine, anyway."

"Did you give any more thought to my offer?" he asked.

"To send Warren home without certain parts of his wardrobe?" I laughed, but I shook my head. "Thanks, anyway, but I don't think I want to go that far."

"If you change your mind . . ." Brad began.

"If you do change your mind, could you wait until

106

Wendy gets out of the hospital and we can both watch?" Meg asked.

I nearly choked on my milk. "Maybe it could be a party theme," I suggested. "Or a new clown act."

Meg considered this. "Nope. We'd scare the little kids."

"Right," I said. I pretended to give consideration to a new idea, though, the way Tina would. "But if nobody's looking, let's reconsider the possibilities."

We laughed so long and hard that everybody in the cafeteria stared at us. Some grinned at us, but others looked at me as if I didn't have a right to enjoy myself.

My smile froze and chipped off. "Sometimes I get tired of trying," I said, more to myself than to Meg and Brad.

"Don't give in," Brad said quickly. "Don't. You'll end up like my sister."

"What do you mean?" I asked.

He shrugged uncomfortably. "She's always afraid, always looking behind her and hurrying. She never laughs anymore."

I thought about what he said during my next class, and decided, then, that I'd see the nurse after school. Maybe she could help. Maybe not.

Meanwhile, I was anxious to learn what had happened between my parents and the principal and Mr. Depard. I could see the principal's closed door when I looked through the glass wall of the office, but there was no way of knowing whether or not Mom and Dad were still in there. I thought of asking Mrs. Camp and decided against it. I even called home to see if Mom and Dad had returned yet, but no one answered the phone. Suspense. Grr, I thought. I was never very good at waiting.

There was still no answer when I called after my last class, so I went to the nurse's office and found her rearranging books on her shelves.

It didn't take long to fill Mrs. Larson in on what had

107

been happening to me. I told her everything but Warren's name. She asked me how I was feeling, how I was sleeping and eating.

"Okay, I guess. I don't think I'm losing weight. At first I couldn't sleep, though. And I have nightmares."

"Bad dreams where you're helpless? Where things are out of your control?"

"How did you know?" I asked.

"Victims of power plays nearly always have dreams like that," she said.

"Power plays?" I asked, bewildered.

"Attempted rape doesn't have anything to do with sex, Amelia," she said. "It has everything to do with power and control. And anger."

I nodded, but I wasn't certain I understood.

"By escaping, you left your attacker with a problem. He still wants to control you."

"And he has," I said, thinking of the humiliation Warren had caused me by lying about me.

Mrs. Larson leaned back in her chair and studied me carefully. "I'm actually surprised that this happened to you," she said. "Usually, assertive girls aren't bothered much. They give off the wrong vibrations. Men looking for power would rather pick on somebody who seems easily frightened and unsure of herself."

I thought about this for a moment. "He caught me off guard," I said. "I was thinking about how good-looking he is and that he's a senior. Then he was late for our date, and I was rattled. You know, embarrassed in front of my family. And he lied to me about other people coming along. I felt uneasy."

"But you were picking up signals that he might not be dependable, right? That he didn't respect you?"

I nodded. "I talked myself out of my suspicions, though."

Mrs. Larson sighed. "Women do that. We make excuses for other people's bad behavior instead of holding them accountable. So we get in trouble."

We talked for a while longer, and then she gave me several pamphlets.

"There are *pamphlets* for this sort of thing?" I asked, shocked.

"You're not the only one in school I've given them to, either," she said sadly. "We're considering passing them out to everyone during the first week of school next year, but there's been opposition to the idea."

"Opposition to learning how to take care of yourself?"

"Opposition to acknowledging that there's a problem that won't go away unless we fight it," she said.

She invited me to come back and talk whenever I felt like it, and added that others did and found that it helped. I wondered if one of the girls she counseled was Franny, who'd tried to tell me she'd never had anything scary happen to her, no, not ever.

How many of us are there?

When I got home, my parents were waiting, and neither of them looked pleased.

"How did things go?" I asked. "Not so good, right?"

"The principal refused to be pinned down about this," Dad said angrily. "He said there's only your word against Warren's, and since the incident happened off school property and after school hours, the school isn't involved."

"But what about Mr. Depard? He was getting involved, except that he's on Warren's side."

"They feel that Warren's school work is affected by the circumstances," Mom said. "That's a direct quote, by the way."

I sat down at the kitchen table, feeling as if my breath had been knocked out. "They still don't believe me."

"I think that they do," Dad said. "But if they admit

it, they'll be committing themselves to working on solutions, and that would involve a lot of time and bother.''

''But they want me to stop talking about Warren, right?'' I said.

''You're doing it at school and it's affecting Warren,'' Mom said. She shook her head disgustedly.

I was furious! I jumped out of my chair and stamped my feet. ''I'll talk about Warren whenever I want to! I'll tell anybody I want to tell!''

I took a good look at my parents' faces and subsided. ''You think I should keep quiet?'' I asked.

''No. You should do whatever you feel like doing,'' Mom said. ''*You* decide. If that inconveniences Warren or anybody else, too bad.''

''We're on your side,'' Dad said. ''Never forget that. Together we're stronger than Warren and the rest of them.''

''Alone I'm stronger than Warren,'' I said quietly.

But I didn't believe that. What I did believe was that Tiny Tina was stronger than Warren, and one way or another she was going to teach him what it was like to keep looking over his shoulder for fear of what might be scuttling along right behind him.

Chapter 14

Incredibly Intelligent Idea No. 14: Did you ever notice that teachers and librarians never need to go to the bathroom? Does that tell you something?

Mogoo, the Mad Magician

Wendy got out of the hospital and the clowns threw her an open house party. Her mother helped her into her Luna Paloona outfit, and Wendy lay propped up on the couch in the family room. For two hours kids came and went, bringing her joke presents and goodies. The rest of us wore our costumes, and we did a spur-of-the-moment performance for Wendy's friends.

"Your crutches could be great in the act," Carl told her. "Even when you don't need them anymore, we could work up a little skit around them."

"She is absolutely not performing with you as long as she's wearing a cast," Wendy's mom said.

"Awww," Wendy groaned. "I've been so bored! And my roommate in the hospital drove me crazy. Can you believe she talked in her sleep? And she told me everything I didn't want to hear about how her boyfriend dumped her . . ."

"Boyfriend?" I asked. "Wendy, I saw her. She must have been ninety-nine years old."

"She had a boyfriend," Wendy insisted. "I saw him. He brought his new girlfriend to the hospital to visit her. . . ."

She stopped talking and looked at me. "In the act, if I had a cast and Mogoo brought you to visit me . . ."

"Oh, it would work!" I cried. "Maybe. After all, Luna dumped Mogoo. How could we work it? Luna would be sorry she lost him. Yes!"

"No!" Mrs. Ingram shouted, but she was laughing. "Only when the cast could be a fake one."

Wendy's first day back at school was an upsetting one for both of us. Miss Lear, outdoing herself, told Wendy in front of the entire class that she might fail because she'd been out of school for so long and hadn't been doing all that well anyway.

"I'll do extra work," Wendy said. I was afraid she was going to pass out from shock and embarrassment.

Miss Lear pretended she didn't hear her.

"Miss Lear?" Wendy asked.

"Why do you insist on having personal conversations in front of everyone?" Miss Lear asked.

"But . . ." Wendy began. Several of the other kids were muttering angrily.

"You started the conversation, Miss Lear," I blurted.

Miss Lear looked at me without blinking.

Tiny Tina took over without any effort on my part at all. "You started it to embarrass Wendy," I said. "I don't believe she's in danger of flunking. You just said that to hurt her because that's what you like doing."

"Go to the office," Miss Lear said.

"I might as well go, too," Wendy said, "because Amelia said exactly what I was thinking."

"Yeah," somebody said. "Right," someone else muttered angrily.

Miss Lear pretended she didn't hear, and as Wendy and I left, she launched into another of her boring lectures.

Mrs. Camp grimaced when the two of us walked through the office door. "Already, Wendy?" she asked. "This is only your first day back."

112

"Maybe we could have a joint meeting with Mr. Depard," I suggested wearily. "It would save time."

Mrs. Camp obliged us by laughing aloud.

Mr. Depard gave us his usual pointless admonitions about being disrespectful and released us. It was almost time for second period, so we spent the extra few minutes at Wendy's locker.

"Never mind Lear," I said. "You look great with a cast. And you swing a mean crutch."

"I hope you're not suggesting that I make them a permanent part of my wardrobe," Wendy said. "Hey, since we're alone, tell me about Mark."

"There's nothing to tell you," I said.

"He looks like there's something he'd like to tell *you*."

"What are you talking about?" I asked.

"Carl says that Mark's getting to like you."

"He always liked me!" I protested.

"You know what I mean."

I hugged myself as if I was warding off a chill. "No, I don't, and I don't want to listen to any more of this."

"Hey! What's the matter with you? What's wrong with Mark? Half the girls in school would love to have him interested in them."

I shook my head. "I don't want anyone thinking about me like that. Maybe getting ideas."

Suddenly I realized that I was beginning to sound like Franny. One of the pamphlets the nurse had given me said that recovery from the shock of an attack would be hampered if the woman let herself think that avoiding men was an answer.

I didn't want to think about any of it! Tiny Tina didn't waste time thinking and pondering and brooding. She just let 'em have it if they pushed her too far.

The bell had rung and we were on our way to our second class. Wendy could make good time on her

113

crutches. What slowed her down was being stopped over and over by kids who were glad to see her back.

Interesting observation: Most of the kids who greeted Wendy didn't say anything to me. If I looked at them, they looked away, embarrassed. I was still the girl who told too much, and I was being punished for it.

I saw Warren several times every day, and when he noticed me, he grinned pityingly. Tiny Tina looked back implacably, while the Amelia inside her cringed.

And once, to my horror, he stopped me and said, "Just between the two of us, I still get a kick out of your tall tales, Amelia."

"I think you're crazy," I said in my Tiny Tina voice. "Really crazy, not just a little bit weird."

He looked around quickly. No one was near us. Suddenly he reached out and grabbed my wrist, twisting it painfully.

"See you around," he whispered.

I watched him strut away, shoulders swinging. I was frozen with fright. The Tiny Tina part of me had vanished completely, and poor baby Amelia had all she could do to keep from crying.

The next time I saw him, he was walking with one of the cheerleaders, his arm around her shoulders, whispering to her and making her laugh. Had she gone out with him yet?

Had she heard what he'd done to me?

Didn't she believe me?

I didn't tell anyone that Warren had twisted my wrist, but I went back to Mrs. Larson that day after school and asked her what I should do if my attacker ever tried to hurt me again.

"Call the police," she said.

"And if no one saw him? We'd be back to his word against mine," I said bitterly.

"Okay," she said, "let's get right down to business. How could he get at you again? Haven't you learned not to let him within ten feet of you? Didn't you read the pamphlet that told you to scream and run?''

''It's embarrassing to do that.''

She looked at me for a long time. "What's worse, a little embarrassment or an attack?''

I was silent.

''Amelia, you can make it too expensive for him to bother you. You don't have to be a victim. Take the aggressive role for your own. Take it! Walk like you know where you're going and intend on getting there. Keep your chin up and swing your arms. Don't sidle away from him and give off panic signals. If he comes too near, make it cost him!''

She was right. Tiny Tina would make him pay for trying to talk to her. For grabbing her wrist.

I thanked the nurse and went home. And on the way, I practiced a new kind of walk.

And then it hit me. That wasn't a new walk. It was my old one. To be my old self, I had to act just as much as I did when I was playing Tiny Tina.

But it was all getting easier, in spite of the momentary setback. I was getting tougher, meaner—exceeding anything Amelia ever would have attempted. Pretty soon it would be second nature to me. A few weeks earlier, before I'd become one of the clowns, Warren's behavior at school would have devastated me beyond recovery. Now a part of me almost wished that Warren would try something again. Tina would wipe up the school with him.

For the next few days, I practiced being Tiny Tina until I woke up feeling like her. Rough. Sassy. She didn't have the vulnerability that let me be a set-up for Warren, that weakness that made me so unsure of myself because he'd been late and lied to me. If he'd come late to Tina's, he'd have found her sitting in front of the TV with a bowl of popcorn, and she'd have told him to buzz off because she didn't want to miss the program. Or maybe she'd have thrown the bowl at him.

I became more self-confident with my part in the clown act. We worked at least twice a week, and I—or rather Tiny Tina—quickly developed a sharp wit. No matter what spontaneous nonsense Mark thought up in his role as Mogoo, the Mad Magician, I was ready for him. More than ready.

And then I went too far.

We had a birthday party engagement one Saturday afternoon, when the first hints of spring made us wish we could spend the day outside instead of in an expensive house that had too much furniture, too many enormous potted plants, and too many spoiled, bored children waiting for us. As soon as we got inside, we must have read each others' minds, because all of us gravitated toward a place where the owner had placed several of these plants, and we began a little chase scene around them.

Mogoo, panting after Tina, his new love, said, "Wait, my little darling, I've got something to ask you." (The kids screamed with laughter at the word "little.")

I stopped trotting away from him and faced him. "I'll ask the questions around here. How about a knuckle sandwich?" (The kids giggled, but Officer Maquick didn't look very happy).

I held up my fist and Mark, as Mogoo, stopped in his tracks. "Oh, please, little love, don't hurt me."

I stepped forward, holding up both fists. "Leave a lady alone, bud, or you'll be carrying your teeth home in a paper sack."

The kids laughed nervously, but Mark backed away immediately, and Carl stepped between us, pretending to arrest Mogoo, claiming that he hadn't paid his rent for a whole year. Meg, as Beano, offered to sell me a pencil with an eraser on both ends. By that time, the little kids hardly knew where to look because so much was going on.

But I was annoyed. I'd been planning on pretending to sock Mogoo, and they'd cut me off. On the way home, while Mrs. MacArthur and Meg were discussing the party food, I asked Mark and Carl why they'd chopped off my act.

Mark shrugged uneasily and didn't say anything.

"Well?" I asked.

"You were coming on too strong," Carl said. His voice was very soft, and I knew his mother couldn't hear him, so I dropped my voice, too.

"What are you talking about? I had a good thing going."

"You were on the verge of scaring the kids," Carl said.

"I don't know what you're talking about," I said.

"Look, Amelia, Mogoo isn't a creep. He's only an off-beat, harmless guy who's tactless, not dangerous. You're getting back at him for what he says. Words, Amelia. It's all just words, not meant to hurt anybody."

"When guys say things like Mogoo says, it's a sign that *they're* coming on strong," I argued. "They've got to be put in their places, right away. Little kids have to learn that."

"This was a birthday party, not a session in self-defense," Carl said. "Amelia, can't you tell the difference between a guy who's just sort of a klutz and one who's dangerous? The kids were supposed to be having a good time, not getting a big scare."

"Well, having a weird magician following you around and . . ." I stopped.

Mark was still wearing his Mogoo clothes and makeup. He looked funny and strange and endearing and harmless.

He *was* funny and strange and endearing and harm-

117

less. It was what he said that bothered me. Those come-ons.

I told the guys that, but they stared at me, not understanding.

"Amelia, Mogoo's always said stuff like that," Mark explained. "He's a big clown. He's not serious. Nobody's in danger, not ever. Luna Paloona answered back with wisecracks and funny insults—she didn't go off the deep end and threaten to hit him. Hitting's out, definitely."

"Officer Maquick chases everybody around with his plastic nightstick," I said.

"But he never hits anybody, and he never even gets close. And he doesn't say threatening things. Can't you see the difference?" Carl was beginning to sound impatient. "Look, Amelia, you can't sound too tough when you're around little kids. It spoils the act."

I sat back in my seat, embarrassed to tears. I was beginning to see what he meant, but I didn't know what else Tiny Tina could do. Did they want more of what Luna Paloona did? She fought off Mogoo with sassy remarks and insults that were mostly jokes.

Had I become Tiny Tina? Or had she become me, with all the rage I had stored up and the desire to hit somebody because of what had been done to me?

I was too confused to think, and I couldn't stop my tears.

"Here, quit that," Mark said, and he pulled me close to him. "If you bawl now, you'll smear your makeup all over both of us. Wait until we're cleaned up, and then you can howl all you want to. Is it a deal?"

I couldn't help laughing. "Deal," I said.

"Then here," he said, and he reached in his pocket. "Take my handkerchief, wipe your eyes and blow your nose." He pulled out a bouquet of awful purple flowers. "Oops, wrong pocket." He reached in another and pulled out a limp toy dog. "Good grief, Oliver's dead!"

118

He handed it to me. "Here, lady, I can't find my handkerchief but maybe this will do."

I doubled up with laughter, and by the time they dropped me off at my house, I felt almost human again.

But when I went to bed that night, I started thinking about Tiny Tina and me again. Which of us had taken over the other?

Chapter 15

Incredibly Intelligent Idea No. 15: Have you ever seen anybody actually using algebra or geometry? Can you imagine calling up a pal and asking him if he wants to go out for pizza and a movie and having him tell you, "Heck no! I'm staying home to calculate how many square inches of chocolate milk my tuba will hold!"

Mogoo, the Mad Magician

The school semester ended with no big surprises. Wendy and I both passed Miss Lear's class, although neither of us got what you might call a spectacular grade. That was the good part. The bad part was that we'd have her again in the spring.

"You'd think she was the only English teacher in school," Wendy complained on the first day of the new semester. She poked her locker with her crutch and it didn't take much imagination to tell that she'd rather have poked Miss Lear.

"At least we don't have her for homeroom this time," I said. "We've got Mrs. Nugent and she's so nice that you could have her for dessert." I stuffed Wendy's umbrella in the back of her locker for her and helped her get organized while I told her my news. "Listen, this will make you laugh. You remember my cousin Erin? Well, she got thrown out of her school in Oregon for painting a mural on the wall."

Wendy grinned. "I take it that this mural wasn't one the school planned on having on that particular wall."

"Actually, from what Erin's grandparents told Mom, it was a really good one, but it made fun of Erin's algebra teacher somehow. They didn't go into any details."

"Well, why didn't the principal just make Erin wash it off?" Wendy asked. "Expelling her seems pretty radical to me."

"It wasn't washable paint," I explained. "And she broke one of the windows to get into the school over the weekend to do it."

Wendy gaped at me. "Oh boy. She is a genuine brat, isn't she?"

"Yes," I said. "I halfway envy her. Can you imagine what she'd do to Miss Lear?"

Wendy grinned. "Is there any possible way we can get her here for a long, long visit?"

I laughed. "My folks have invited her to come every summer and every spring break since her parents died, but she doesn't want to. Heather's mother has invited her a dozen times, too."

"Doesn't she like you and Heather anymore?"

I shrugged. "I guess not. But when we were little, we used to spend lots of time together."

"Things change," Wendy said. "And losing her parents was such an awful thing. I remember that day—we all went to Patty Murphy's party. And afterward, everybody's folks came to take them home except Erin's. They'd been in the accident and nobody knew yet."

I blinked hard. I couldn't remember that afternoon without wanting to cry all over again. Poor Erin had waited and waited on the front porch, until finally Patty's mother called her back in the house and began phoning around to find out what had happened to Uncle David and Aunt Kathy. It was late in the evening before anybody learned that Erin's parents had died. She didn't even get to say good-bye to them.

I cleared my throat. "Well, Erin's a wonderful artist, her grandparents say. But she's a terror at school, and at home, too, sometimes."

"What's going to happen to her?" Wendy asked.

"I don't know. Maybe I'll write to her again and see if she'll answer me this time."

Mark wandered up and interrupted the conversation by presenting each of us with a large, sticky bun from the cafeteria. "Breakfast," he said. "Not airline food, either." He nudged Wendy. "I saw you halfway running yesterday after school. How much longer before you get the cast off?"

"I'm going to rip it off myself if I can't get out of it pretty soon," Wendy said. "I miss clowning with you guys, and I need the money, too."

"Oh, I'm getting rich," I said. "The little guys are always after me for treats and comic books now. And Jamie's figured out a way I can lend his grade school friends money and charge interest."

"That kid's going far in the business world," Mark said. He draped his arm over my shoulder. "Are you ready for Saturday?"

The clowns were performing again in a few days, at a new mall opening up on the other side of Lake Washington. We'd be seen by the biggest crowd yet, and the MacArthurs were hoping that our appearance there would generate lots of new business.

"I'm so ready that I can't wait," I told Mark. "Mom added some new stuffing to my costume, so I look like a giant."

"Yum yum," Mark said, in Mogoo's voice. "I love a pretty lady who's so big I almost can't get my arms around her."

"Quit that," I said. Kids passing by were watching us. "I've invented a new tattoo that you'll love." I held

122

out my arm and demonstrated where I'd draw it. "Right here I'll have a big heart, and then I'll draw a spider crawling over it."

"Oh, yuck," Wendy said. "Where do you come up with these ideas?"

"I don't," I said truthfully. "Tina does. And isn't that tattoo exactly what she'd have? Something awful and ugly."

"But Mogoo only loves her more," Mark said, and then, before I could say anything else, he trotted off with a backward wave and joined a couple of his friends farther down the hall.

"He's crazy about you," Wendy said.

"He's crazy period," I grumbled.

The bell rang and we went off to Mrs. Nugent's class, to enjoy ourselves in first period for a change.

To my surprise, the senior cheerleader I'd seen Warren with was sitting in front of the class. She glanced up when we came in, then looked away. Her cheeks turned scarlet, as if she'd just been slapped.

"Hi, Shannon," Wendy said to her. But the girl either didn't hear or she pretended that she didn't.

"I wonder what's wrong with her?" Wendy asked as we took our seats in the back.

"I didn't know you knew her," I said.

"Her mother is Mom's hairdresser," Wendy said.

"And she's interested in art?" I asked. "I've never had her in a class."

"She used to be interested—I suppose she's just filling in her schedule with any old elective where there's an opening. Boy, she sure didn't want to face you, did she? Maybe she's finally figured out what a jerk Warren is."

"Maybe," I said slowly. "Or maybe she found out the hard way."

I had trouble concentrating during the class. I found

123

myself looking at Shannon again and again and wondering about her.

Well, she should have believed what she heard about Warren, I thought suddenly. I could feel myself filling up with anger again.

Warren, Warren! He always won. There was no end to it.

On Friday after school, while I was helping Mimi and Cassie clean out their closet, Mark surprised me by stopping by the house.

I let him in and apologized for how I looked—the little guys had amused themselves by plastering me with their old sticker collection.

"Nice," he said as he peeled a star off my forehead. "But I don't think I care much for the slice of watermelon stuck to your chin."

I removed that sticker and laughed. "What can I do for you, Mark? Do you want to talk about the clowns?"

Mark looked uncomfortable. "Maybe. A little. I wanted to be sure we were in agreement about how far Tina would go tomorrow when she and Mogoo are arguing."

"We'll be performing in front of little kids, as well as adults and teenagers," I said. "I'm not going to scare anybody."

"No heavy stuff," Mark said gently. "Okay?"

My face burned. "Give me a break," I said. "I got the message when Carl talked to me. I'm not going to hit Mogoo. Or even threaten to. Okay?"

Mark looked as embarrassed as I was. "I hate this conversation," he said.

"Then why are we having it?"

"Because I really like you and I care about what happens to you. So do the other clowns."

"You've been talking about me behind my back?" I cried. "How could you do that?"

"It's because we hate seeing you so hurt and so changed," he said.

"I didn't do this to myself," I said. "Warren did it!"

Mark looked straight at me. "How long are you going to let that slob be a part of your life?"

"He's not!" I cried.

"He is. You're giving him time and attention that he doesn't deserve."

I covered my face with my hands. "I don't know how to stop thinking about him. I would if I could." I looked up at Mark again. "Can't you see that?"

"I see that you'd like to fight him by his own rules," Mark said.

"I don't know what you're talking about." I could hear Mimi and Cassie upstairs, arguing about something. At least they weren't listening to this, but I didn't know how much more privacy Mark and I would have. And I wasn't all that sure I wanted to go on with the conversation.

"I think Warren would be flattered if he knew how much he had managed to change you," Mark said. "Every time I see the guy, I want to punch out his lights. But right now it's more important to me that you wake up and see what you're letting happen to you. It shows in the clown act. You want to win. You want to put Mogoo down so bad that he can't get back up again. You really want to hurt him. It's getting close to not being funny anymore, Amelia. If you want to get even with Warren, I can't blame you. But the way to do it isn't by scaring a lot of little kids."

I shook my head in frustration. Why couldn't he understand? "Why don't you guys fire me then? Maybe you should, if you think I'm spoiling the act."

"Because you can be so funny. Silly funny. Remember how you and Heather used to be? You kept everybody in the cafeteria laughing. That's what we want to see. Not this hard-line stuff." He put his big, warm hands on my shoulders. "Can't you leave Warren out of it? If you want me to, I'll round up a couple of the guys and we'll take Warren for a ride down an alley that he won't forget. I'd do it if you could put an end to this anger of yours."

"But you don't think that's the way to really fix Warren, do you?" I asked.

He shook his head soberly. "No. I think the cops could have taught him something." He held up his hands, warding off my protest. "I know, I know. It's late for that now. And you think you wouldn't be believed. But that would have been the best way. Now we have to deal with what we've got. And we've got a clown act that isn't always so funny—and a girl who's too angry all the time. Can't we work out a way to fix both of them?"

I sat down abruptly on the hall chair. "Okay. How? You have to tell me exactly how."

"What happened to the goofy sense of humor you used to have? Remember all the tricks and jokes you and Heather—and the rest of us—used to pull on each other? Can't we get some of that back? For the act—and for yourself, too."

"Nothing's funny to me anymore," I said, and I got up, intending to open the door for him. I didn't want to talk to him.

But he wound his arms around me and held me tight. "Please," he whispered. "Don't get lost."

Lost. That's what I'd been. Lost to myself.

"Does Mom know you let Mark hug you?" Cassie demanded from the head of the stairs.

Mark jumped away from me as if he'd been stuck with a pin.

"Cassie, go help Mimi with the closet," I said.

"We did our closet!" Cassie cried. "We did ours and then we did your . . ."

"Mine?" I yelled. "You got into my closet?"

"Is this going to be a war or only an argument?" Mark asked.

"It's war," I said, heading for the stairs. "I'll think about what you said, Mark, but right now I've got to rescue my stuff."

"Do you still want this nightshirt?" Cassie asked, holding up a hideous old shirt with a picture of Batman on it that I hadn't worn since fourth grade. "The dogs have been sleeping on it."

"Give me that!" I shouted, running after her.

Behind me, I heard Mark laugh, and then the front door shut.

It took me an hour to straighten up the mess the little guys had made of my closet—and my drawers and my desk. By that time, I wasn't so embarrassed about the conversation I'd had with Mark.

But I wasn't able to really think about what he'd said until I went to bed that night. I had so much on my mind that I ended up getting out of bed again and writing a lot of things down on paper, just so I could get my head straight about them.

Fact: Warren was just plain evil, and calling him anything else wasn't facing up to the truth.

Fact: He'd hurt me in more ways that I'd ever realized, because he'd changed my personality.

Fact: I wasn't Tiny Tina and she wasn't Amelia. She was a tough character, but she was supposed to be funny, and I had to learn to keep her that way and not slip into that meanness that had become so satisfying to me.

Fact: If I was ever going to get even with Warren, I'd have to play by my own rules, not his. But that didn't mean I couldn't win.

Fact: I had to stop letting Warren occupy my mind and attention. He'd had all of my life he was going to get during those awful moments in the alley. The rest of it was mine.

Fact: Maybe I'd never feel the same way again about the people I knew who hadn't supported me and believed me. But I wasn't going to let that take over my life, either. Maybe it was good for me to learn who my real friends were.

The next morning, Saturday, I woke up full of enthusiasm for the clown act at the new mall. I went over and over in my mind the funniest responses I could make to Mogoo's crush on Tiny Tina, remembering to keep a light touch, a light and very silly touch. Play it for laughs, Amelia, I told myself over and over. Mogoo isn't Warren.

I went down to breakfast a little late, to find my parents sitting at the table staring at each other while my sisters and Jamie stuffed themselves with pancakes.

"You guys look like you'd just seen a TV news break about the end of the world," I said.

Mom nodded soberly. "You're close."

"So?" I asked. "Is something wrong? What's going on?"

"Guess what?" Jamie said. "Mom and Dad got a phone call. Erin's coming to stay with us."

"Next weekend," Mimi added. "That's eleventy-seven days from now."

"That's seven days from now," Dad said. "Barely time to hide the silver and buy a watchdog."

"Jock," Mom said, with a warning look. She smiled at me, a little weakly. "Erin's grandmother isn't well and it seems that she simply can't manage the girl any longer. So we invited her to stay with us."

"What did she do this time?" I asked, fascinated.

"Don't ask," Mom said. "What time are you leaving for the mall?"

"Quick change of subject," I muttered as I poured juice for myself. "I'm leaving at nine."

"Then you'd better start getting your gear together," Dad said.

"Hold the boat," I said. A thought had just occurred to me. "There are four bedrooms in this house. And six people. Where is Erin going to sleep?"

"We'll bring down that old twin bed in the attic," Dad said. "The one Heather uses when she's here."

"And put it where?" I asked, already dreading the answer.

"Where else?" Mom said. "Your room. She certainly can't sleep with Jamie, and every other bedroom is full up."

"I get to have the family beast in my room?" I asked. "As if I didn't already have enough trouble."

"Do you mind so terribly?" Mom said. "I know this is a bad time for you . . ."

"No, it isn't," I said crossly. "It's practically an everyday, ordinary time, but I still don't know if I can face up to Erin the Awful painting murals on my walls and breaking my windows."

"She sounds great to me," Jamie said, his mouth full.

"We'll try it and do the best we can for her," Dad said. "If it doesn't work out, then we'll try something else. But she's got to have somebody, and right now we're the only somebodies she has left."

I gobbled down a quick breakfast and ran back upstairs to get my costume ready. Warren. Erin. What next?

Think *funny*, I told myself.

The MacArthurs picked me up in their van a few minutes later. A small back room had been set aside for us at the mall, so we changed our clothes there and helped each other with makeup.

"How are you feeling?" Mark asked me.

"Funny, I hope," I told him. "I had a great idea last night. When you give me the flowers this time, tell me that they came from a far-off land."

"Okay, a far-off land. Then what?" Mark stuck his red nose on and adjusted it in the mirror I was holding for him.

"I'll say that they look like you picked them yourself and brought them back the long way around. Then I'll stuff them in your hat."

"My hat's got that old blue Easter bunny of my brother's in it."

"Hmm. I know what!" Meg cried. She babbled through another idea that sounded good, and before we knew it, we'd added another great bit to the act.

"I wish Wendy were here," Carl said.

"She'll be with us soon," I said.

"Lots of kids from school will be here to watch," Meg said.

My heart missed a beat, but then I remembered that I'd be hidden inside Tiny Tina and didn't need to worry about people staring at me, Amelia. Sure, they'd know who I was, but it was easier for me when I was in costume and makeup.

But then, the other kids said that it was easier for them, too.

Mrs. MacArthur came to get us a few minutes later, saying that the master of ceremonies was ready to introduce us.

"Break a leg," Mark said, and he pinched my fake nose. "And don't let me forget to get you a new nose. That one's cracked."

"I think it's perfect," I said. "Who else but Tina would have a crack on her nose?"

As usual, I was halfway through the act before I really got control of my stage fright. We'd already done the flower bit and were warming up to the place where Beano gets his arms caught in his coat sleeves, and Mo-

130

goo, trying to help him, gets his own arms caught, when I looked over the edge of the stage and saw Warren.

For a moment, I felt like I was back in the alley again, trying to get away from him, and I was so frightened that I couldn't breathe.

I've got to get out of here, I thought. Right now! Before he does something to me.

Chapter 16

Incredibly Intelligent Ideas No. 16 a, b, and c:
Shoelaces only break when you're in a hurry.
Buttons only come off when it can embarrass
you. You only sneeze when you don't have a
handkerchief.

Mogoo, the Mad Magician

Did Warren recognize me? I didn't know. For an instant, he and I seemed to be frozen, staring at each other. But then he looked away from me and watched Mogoo instead, with even more interest.

He saw us as clowns, not as kids from his school. I was safe, hiding inside Tina. I didn't need to run. But I couldn't seem to catch my breath and my hands were like ice.

Mogoo and Beano, pretending to be hopelessly entangled in Beano's coat sleeves, blundered in my direction, just as we'd planned. I concentrated on my part in the skit and grabbed the flapping sleeves. In an instant, I had them tied around Mogoo, trapping him and Beano together. Office Maquick circled them, shaking his nightstick. The crowd laughed.

I glanced at Warren. He was looking at me again and grinning. Didn't he recognize me yet? A boy moved up next to him—a stranger—and said something. Both of them laughed.

I hated Warren, and I hated him most of all when he was laughing. Mogoo, Beano, and Officer Maquick were still bumbling together. Beano was standing on the tip of one of Officer Maquick's huge shoes. The shoe came off, revealing a long orange sock with a plastic toe sticking out of the end of it.

I looked back at Warren and caught him watching me. His smile faltered a little. He recognized me now, and he was surprised for an instant. Then he smiled and his eyes glinted. I was so panicked that my ears buzzed.

What would he do? I couldn't bear being humiliated in front of all these people. Why did he always seem to have all the power over every situation I found myself in with him? Why couldn't I ever take charge, and make something turn out right for me? And now, even worse, my friends were involved. I couldn't let Warren spoil their act just because he wanted to torment me again.

But suddenly I knew what to do, and my panic dropped away. Make it too expensive for him to bother you, Mrs. Larson had told me. Take the aggressive role yourself.

I leaned over the edge of the stage and beckoned to him. "Come here, gorgeous boy," I said in Tina's raucous voice.

Annoyed, Warren shook his head. It didn't take much imagination to see that he resented the attention of someone as enormous, ugly, and ridiculous as Tiny Tina. Probably he'd wanted to make fun of me. Now, all of a sudden, I'd started something that perhaps *he* wouldn't be able to finish.

We had the attention of the people nearest him and some of them laughed.

"Aw," I crooned. "Won't you come a little nearer? I'd like to get a close look at a handsome fellow like you. Come on. Step up here."

A girl standing behind Warren gave him a little push. "Go on," she said, laughing. "See what she wants."

"Oh, I want *him*," I said to her. "Don't you think we'd look cute together?" I beckoned to Warren again.

133

"Hey, sweetie, come here and give us a big kiss." The crowd roared with laughter.

Warren's face burned red. "Leave me alone," he said. He moved back, as if he wanted to leave, but the boy next to him, the stranger, grabbed his arm and tugged him toward the stage.

"Come on, be a good sport," the boy said.

Most of the crowd was watching me, now. I had no idea what Mogoo and Beano were doing, but Officer Maquick, pointing at me, was dancing the little, goofy shuffle he did when other clowns had center stage.

I knelt down at the edge of the platform. "That's right, drag that pretty boy right up here where I can reach him," I said. "My, my, just look at his eyelashes! They're the longest ones I've ever seen!"

Warren tried to smile. I was sure he wanted to pretend that none of this mattered, but he couldn't pull it off. The crowd had closed in behind him and he was trapped. I reached out my hand.

"Come here, honey," I crooned. "I want to spend some time with you, getting acquainted."

Warren looked furious now. Did he recognize the words he'd once said to me?

"I love looking into your eyes," I said. "I think you should go to a movie with me. I can promise you a real good time. Wouldn't you like that? Just you and me? Nobody else. And afterward—oh, boy, I'll take you to a terrific place I know."

The crowd was laughing, but Warren seemed ready to explode.

"What's the matter, honey?" I asked. "Scared to be alone with Tiny Tina? Aaaaw. Poor little boy. I won't let anything bad happen to you. I sure wouldn't do what other girls do. You know. Jump out of your car and let you drive home all alone in the dark. Good old Tina'll just boost you up on the back of her motorcycle and take you to some romantic place. You'll love it. So relax, honey. Relax."

I reached out my hands to him but he wouldn't touch them. The crowd yelled, "Go ahead! Get up on the stage. She likes you. Be a sport. Go on!"

I wiggled my fingers. "Come on. You're safe. I won't let the boogie man get you. Get right up here beside me and show me what you've got."

"Go on! Go on!" the crowd shouted. But Warren turned and pushed himself roughly through the crowd. In a moment he was out of sight.

But the boy he'd been standing beside leaped up nimbly beside me. "If he won't, I will!" he said.

"Stop!" Mogoo, the Mad Magician shouted. "He can't have you, Tina. You're meant for me and only me."

The boy was quick-witted. "Not anymore," he said, and he tried to put his arms around me, but Tina was too big for that.

"Don't touch her," Mogoo shouted. "She's the love of my life."

The boy was enjoying himself so much that I found myself enjoying him, too. "He looks pretty good to me, Mogoo," I said.

"But I can't get my arms around you," the boy panted. "There's just too much of you."

"Not for me," Mogoo said. He twirled his cape and pulled out a wand. "Get away from her or I'll cast a spell on you and turn you into a toad."

The boy looked down at himself. "Gee, the girl I asked to dance last night told me I was already a toad."

The crowd screamed with laughter, but they weren't so noisy that I missed hearing Mogoo say, "If you're interested in a job, see us after the show."

The boy muttered, "Wish I could, but I've got two jobs already." He jumped off the stage, blew me kisses, and disappeared.

Mogoo pulled a bundle of dried weeds out of a pocket and handed them to me. "Take these, love, and follow me."

Tina pretended to consider the offer. "I just might," I said in her voice. "But that first boy was pretty cute. Maybe I should run after him and see if he's changed his mind about me."

"I think he might have," Mogoo said, and he laughed harder than the crowd.

We finished our skit a little late because of the new material we'd added, and the applause went on so long that I almost got tired bowing. Almost, but not quite.

In the changing room, Mark and Meg danced me around in circles until I was out of breath. "You did it, you did it!" Meg shouted. "You made that creep look like a total idiot."

"Why, what a thing to say," I said, grinning. "All I did was repeat back to him the things he'd said to me. I can't understand why he didn't want to go out with me. After all, look at what I promised him. A real good time."

"I think he didn't believe you," Carl said.

"Maybe he's heard that line before," Meg said.

Mark grinned down at me. "Maybe he wishes he'd never used it in the first place."

Suddenly I didn't feel like laughing anymore. "I don't think I taught him anything. He won't stop what he's been doing to girls."

Mark pulled me close in spite of Tina's padding. "That's not your fault. You did everything you could. But one thing for sure, he won't bother you again. You really embarrassed him."

"I wish I'd realized before that I had the power to do it—to make him shut up and leave me alone whenever I wanted." I pulled off my leather aviator's cap and then my bushy wig.

"You were too scared to see how much control you

136

had over the situation," Meg said. "My dad told me once that getting control over a bad situation depends on if you can actually see yourself doing it first."

"I could never see myself doing anything but running away," I told my friends. "Until now. Gee, I wish I learned a long time ago how useful a big mouth can be."

"Help," Mark said, laughing. "I think we're all in trouble."

I didn't get home until after my family had already eaten dinner, but Mom had saved plenty of food for me. I told my parents what had happened while I stuffed myself with warmed-over roast beef.

Dad shook his head, but he was laughing. "He'll keep his distance from you now," he said. "He never expected that you'd turn on him in public. But I still wish . . ."

Mom put her hand on his arm. "I know. So do I. This probably won't cure him."

"But the problem's out in the open," I said. "At least people know what he did to me, and if they don't believe me, then there's nothing I can do about it. I did the best I could."

"He might continue to make problems for you at school with your counselor," Dad said, scowling.

I grinned. "Oh, I'm not worried about Mr. Depard. In one week Erin will be here, and then he'll find out what real trouble is."

My parents laughed, but Mom looked close to crying at the same time. "I don't think we should joke about Erin's problems," she said.

"Sorry," I said. "I guess what's going to happen to Mr. Depard isn't really funny, but I'm sure that if he ever said anything as stupid to Erin as he said to me, she'd know exactly how to handle him."

"Heaven help us all," Dad said, but then he grinned again. "I just remembered what Erin did to the boy who

137

stole her wallet. Do you suppose Warren might make the mistake of talking to her?''

''I doubt it, but I'm not going to warn him off,'' I said, laughing. I heard the phone ringing, and then Jamie came in to tell me that Mark was calling me.

''Would you like to go to a movie?'' he asked. ''I promise that we won't park anyplace afterward except in front of your house.''

''Better be careful with Tiny Tina,'' I said, giggling. ''I suppose you're going to tell me next that we're going to be alone, too.''

''No, actually I was about to say that Wendy, her cast, and Carl will meet us at the theater.'' Mark was laughing under his breath.

''If they don't show up, you're in trouble,'' I told him.

''I know,'' he said. ''I want to stay on your good side, so I'm bringing you a present.''

''What is it?''

''Wait and see,'' he said. ''I'll pick you up at seven-thirty.''

The movie was wonderful, Wendy and Carl really were there, and we all went out for pizza afterward. I kept asking Mark what his present was, but he wouldn't tell me until at last he'd taken me home and we were sitting in his car at the curb.

''Are you ready?'' he asked.

''I was ready hours ago,'' I complained.

Mark took a square box out of the glove compartment and handed it to me. I pulled off the lid and lifted out a shiny, new, red plastic nose.

''Your other one looks awful,'' he said. ''So I got you this. And I got myself one that matches.'' He reached into the glove compartment and pulled out another nose, then popped it on. ''Try yours,'' he said.

I fumbled around and finally got it on.

"That's on upside down," Mark said. "You'll drown in the rain when you get out of the car."

"It's not upside down," I said. "Oh, yes it is. Oops. How's this?"

"Wonderful. You look ridiculous, and that's the whole point. You're becoming a better clown than the rest of us put together, you know that?"

I shook my head. "I don't believe it. But I'll never be able to thank all of you enough for letting me join the troupe. Sometimes I thought that my entire life was going to be one long, depressing, rainy day. I had always been friendly with practically everybody in school, so I expected them to support me after—well, you know. But I finally figured out that only brave people are able to support others. And you guys were the brave ones."

"Not like you," Mark said. He pulled me close to him and rested his head against mine.

"I'm worn out with resenting the ones who let me down so hard. I guess I should feel sorry for them, even Mr. Depard and Miss Lear."

"That's all right," Mark said. "Think of all the fun you'll have doing horrible things to them."

"I don't really have time to do anything horrible to anybody. We've got two parties to clown around at tomorrow and one Monday night. And didn't I tell you? My cousin Erin is coming to stay. She gets here in a few days. I absolutely don't have a spare minute, not even to murder Miss Lear."

"Do you have time for me?" Mark asked.

He tried to kiss me but we bumped clown noses. "I have exactly one million years for you," I told him.

"That's almost enough," he said as he pulled off our big plastic noses. Our own noses were exactly the right size.